THE SUMMER BREAK

MEGAN REINKING

Editing by Jenn Lockwood

Proofreading and Interior Formatting by Yours Truly Book Services

Cover Design by IndieSage

This book is dedicated to the Bookstagram community and the many friends I've made there. Saying thank you for your support and excitement for my books doesn't seem like enough. Every single comment, share and review truly means the world to me. I hope you love Matt and Paige as much as I do.

1

PAIGE

Three more hours. Three more hours. I repeat those words in my head, staring at the whiteboard in front of me. I inhale a deep breath just as another paper airplane comes whizzing past my ear, crashing into the whiteboard and falling to the ground next to my heel. It's pretty symbolic of the state of my classroom right now, which is utterly chaotic.

"Whoops. Sorry, Miss C!" Brady Heinz huffs out as he rushes past me in a blur, grabbing his airplane on the way. The classroom is loud and buzzing with excitement. My second-graders are fully enjoying our end-of-the-year party.

Alright, I'll admit, I'm enjoying it, too—I love my students and our daily life at school. I'm just also desperately in need of that clock to turn to 2:15 p.m. so I can pack up my things and officially close the door on this school year. The excitement of summer has already started and has been buzzing for the past few weeks, actually. It's time to put the kids—and myself, if I'm honest—out of our misery and let them loose for the summer.

Three more hours.

"Okay, friends, find your seats, please!"

A few children find their seats immediately, while others are dragging their feet like I just asked them to walk the plank or something, but honestly, I can relate. I'm over the rules and structure of daily school life, too. I need summer break just as much as my kids do at this point. We're all mentally checked out, just going through the motions to finish out the day as best we can.

"I know it's the last day of school, but we still need to be good listeners and follow the rules," I remind them.

Millie Bradley nods her head in agreement, hands neatly folded across her desk, while Jackson Peters is the last one to find his seat, which is par for the course for him. He drops down with a sigh, slouching in his chair, his mouth twisting up in an annoyed smirk.

He's been one of the most challenging students I've had so far in my three years of teaching. He's a good kid overall, but he lacks discipline at home, which ultimately carries over into the classroom—constantly being defiant against school procedures and expectations, pushing back on everything I say, seeing what he can get away with. He's needed a good dose of tough love and clear boundaries this year, which I have had no problem with and happily gave him.

I find my stride as a teacher when I need to put a little extra thought into the best way to get through to a student. We've had an interesting dynamic this year, Jackson and I. After quite a bit of back and forth and several behavior interventions, we've settled into a comfortable, co-existing, teacher-student relationship. I try my best to advance his education in a subtle, non-confrontational way, while he tones down his behavior, rarely causing a widespread classroom disruption anymore like he did in the fall.

I scan the classroom to find twenty-one sets of eight-year-old eyeballs staring expectantly at me, but not everyone is still. Shoes are tapping on the floor, and fingernails are drumming on the desks. Enthusiastic energy from the party shifts and settles into the familiar buzz of impatience and moodiness that always occurs right before lunch. A party high plus low blood sugar does not make for a good combination. These kids need to eat.

"Let's set a timer for the next five minutes and clean up before we can line up and head to lunch. I know we just had a super-fun party, but let's remember to keep it together and settle down while we straighten up," I say.

I set the timer and turn on some relaxing music to hopefully help calm their little bodies. The next several minutes are spent collecting trash from the floor and tidying up the classroom. It always amazes me how quickly desks can get shifted and chairs can wind up tipped over.

I'm all of a sudden regretting my idea for the make-your-own kaleidoscope craft we did during the party. Sequins, glitter, and leftover stickers almost completely cover the floor, and I carefully peel a strip of craft tape out of my hair.

After the room is in decent shape and my students are lined up and quiet, we walk down to the lunchroom. I pass them off to the lunchroom monitors and then head back to my desk. Most days, I eat in the staff lounge with the other teachers, but today I plan to eat in my room so I can vacuum and clear out my desk a little bit —get a head start on my classroom checklist before the day's over.

As I take a bite of my salad, my mind drifts to my list of things I need to do before I leave in two days. Tomorrow will be another day spent cleaning out my classroom, followed by one last trip to Target, but the day after that, I leave for Hawaii to spend the summer there.

My best friend, Mia, moved to Honolulu a little over a year ago to be with her boyfriend, John. I've visited them a few times, but it's been about six months since I've been able to make it over there, and I desperately miss it. Hawaii has a way of consuming your very being. Once you get a taste of paradise, it's all you can think about until you can experience it again. At least, that's how it is with me. I'm dying to get back there.

Now that I have the summer off, I'll be able to spend a full two months there, and I am beyond excited. The vision of sipping a Mai Tai on the beach under the warm sun has gotten me through some pretty long Minnesota winter days. I finish eating my salad and manage to get quite a bit of purging done before my students arrive back from lunch.

As they're filing in the door, I hear, "Miss C, did you know that you kind of look like a cow today? You're wearing all black and white!"

I stifle a laugh. Some might take offense to that remark, but it doesn't faze me. Comes with the territory of working with kids, I suppose. Every teacher has a list a mile long of the crazy things kids have said to them.

"That's exactly what I was going for, Claire!"

She gives me a nod of approval and continues on to her cubby while I smile, knowing how much I'm going to miss being ragged on by my students. I think my ability to find the humor in every situation and not get stressed too easily is part of what makes me a good teacher. Plus, I have a pretty impressive sarcastic side, which doesn't please my mother very much but comes in handy at school. I'm able to dish it right back to my students—within reason, of course.

I spend the next couple hours completely present with my students, doing fun, last-day-of-school activities and appreciating each and every one of them. I will miss seeing their little faces every day. As much as I'm ready for the summer, I truly enjoy teaching with all my heart, and I get attached to my students. Saying goodbye at the end of the year is hard.

I help gather lunch boxes and stuff any remaining artwork and homework into backpacks. After the children had all high-fived and raced out of the classroom to their buses, I let out a deep breath, allowing myself to feel grateful for this school year —difficult students and all.

Then, I smile to myself, mentally wrapping a nice little bow around this year, and start gathering boxes to take to my car. I have an impressive collection of end-of-the-year gifts, so it takes me two trips to load everything into my car. I leave a few things on my desk for tomorrow, grab my purse, and shut my door.

I feel the heat from the sun on my cheek once I step outside and smile. The last few weeks, we've had absolutely beautiful weather here in Minnesota. Sometimes, summer comes early, and I'm grateful that we've had several beautiful, sunny, seventy-degree days. When I booked the Hawaii trip, a tiny part of me was bummed about missing a whole summer here. Us Minnesotans tend to soak up the nice weather as much as we can before the seasons change all too quickly, so this gorgeous weather has been great.

My chest tightens with a pang of sadness at the thought of missing out on my favorite things that I usually do in the summer. Checking out different bike and hiking trails is something I always look forward to doing, not to mention the countless weekends I spend at friends' cabins. But I remind myself that I usually do all of those things with Mia, so it wouldn't be a typical summer even if I stayed. I also love going to brunch anywhere with an outdoor patio—bonus points if it overlooks a lake. Luckily, I squeezed in a few brunch dates with the girls in the last couple weeks, so I got my waffles-and-mimosa fix before I leave.

Sliding my sunglasses over my eyes, I drive out of the school parking lot, turning right to drive the three blocks to my apartment. When I was offered this teaching job a few years ago, I moved across town to the city of Plymouth to be closer to the school. It's convenient being only about ten minutes away, especially during the winter when the roads can be pretty slick and snow-covered.

Twisting my key into the lock, I push my apartment door open just as my phone starts ringing in my purse. I'm carrying a box with a variety of mugs, candles, and plants—all with some variation of *The Best Teacher Ever* or *#1 Teacher* on them, so I slide the box carefully onto my kitchen counter, then rummage for my phone.

"Hey, Mia!" I can't help the smile that forms on my face. Man, do I miss my best friend. She's like my own personal ray of sunshine. She never fails to put a smile on my face no matter what kind of mood I'm in.

"Hey, gorgeous! Are you all packed up and ready for the best summer of your life?" she asks.

"Almost. I have everything in piles on the floor. I just need to put it all in my suitcase... ugh, I'm soo ready to be there!"

"Me, too! I have your room all ready for you. Eek, I'm so excited! Oahu's not gonna know what hit it. We'll spend every single day together, going on adventures. It'll be like 'Paige and Mia's Summer Break Through the States'," she laughed, referring to the summer I spent five weeks road-tripping with her family through North Dakota, Montana, South Dakota, and back up through southern Minnesota.

"Except, we're adults now, and we'll be in Hawaii, sipping daiquiris, not in grade school with your parents on a mission to find a 'Greetings From' postcard in every city we pass through," I laugh.

John and Mia have a separate cottage on their property, but it's pretty much booked solid through the summer, so I'll be staying with them in their guest room, which is perfectly fine with me. I would stay in a tent on the beach if it meant I'd wake up in Hawaii every day.

I'm not picky.

"What are you up to?" I ask, making small talk while I ponder what to pack first.

"Just got back from the beach, getting ready to go out for dinner tonight. We're meeting up with Matt and Brian later, too. Oh, by the way," she chuckles, "I'm not the only one excited that you're coming. Matt is absolutely a smitten kitten. He lights up every time your name gets brought up. I don't think he knows how obvious it is," she says, stifling another giggle.

"Oh boy, seriously? Still?" Matt is John's good friend. He's cocky, a little over the top, and loves being the center of attention. Granted, he does have the looks to back it up—and the muscles—but that's beside the point.

He's tried making a move on me every single time I've visited, but I haven't given in. I've personally witnessed him flirting with an obscene number of women, mostly when he's working one of his bartending shifts, and I have no interest in being just another number to him.

All the flirting with other women doesn't stop him from shooting his shot with me, though. Every single time, without fail.

It doesn't really bother me. I'm always happy to put him in his place. He's the kind of guy you need to be direct with, giving clear intentions and boundaries, much like Jackson Peters. Luckily, he's given me plenty of practice this year, so dealing with Matt shouldn't be a big deal. It's not lost on me how comical it is that I'm comparing Matt to a second-grader.

Hey, if the shoe fits.

"Yup," she says, "might have to put that boy on a leash when you get here." She laughs.

"Eh, I can handle myself."

"Yes, you can," she agrees, "and he's not so bad once you get to know him. He's a good guy once you cut through all the arrogance."

I snort. "Just the kind of guy I'm looking for..."

Mia giggles in my ear as I slide my suitcase out from under my bed, assessing my piles of clothes and summer items laid out on the floor.

"Okay, how many swimsuits are too many swimsuits?" I ponder, lifting a stack of them to count.

"No such thing. Bring them all," she says.

I settle on four suits and lay them in the suitcase.

"What about sunglasses?"

"I've never found myself wishing I had fewer pairs."

"You're gonna be no help here, aren't you?"

"Probably not. I say bring it all!" She laughs, which in turn, makes me laugh.

"Okay, I'm gonna let you go so I can actually get some packing done tonight. I have a final faculty meeting at school in the morning, and then I need to finish clearing out my classroom, and I won't have much time after that. But I'll call you tomorrow, okay?"

"Alright, can't wait to see you! Bye!"

I hang up and toss my phone onto my bed, focusing my attention back on my suitcase. Each pile of clothes that I manage to squeeze in has me feeling more and more excited about this trip. I'm in major need of a break, and spending a relaxing vacation in paradise with my best friend and no eight-year-olds in sight sounds heavenly.

2

MATT

The smack of a pillow on my cheek brings me out of my sleepy haze. Pushing my eyes open, I blink a few times until the blurry figure hovering over my bed becomes my sister, Tori.

"Rise and shine, Sleeping Beauty. Do you know what time it is?" she asks, tossing a couple clothes from the floor into the hamper.

I roll over, bringing a pillow over my face to block out the light.

Ugh.

Not again.

"Nope," I grunt, my voice muffled against the pillow.

"It's 11:15. You're wasting the day! Come on, I started coffee for you."

I sigh and push the covers off. There's no point in resisting her. She's relentless. Tori is one of my four sisters. At just twenty months younger, she's the closest sibling to me in age. We were often mistaken as twins growing up, and we've always been pretty close. Ava, Grace, and Emily are my other sisters, all older than Tori and me.

All four of them are overbearing and have absolutely no boundaries when it comes to me—constantly showing up unannounced at my apartment, cooking for me, and giving unsolicited advice about my life. I gave up trying to fight it a long time ago. I accepted the fact that this is just how my life is back when I was six, sitting in a chair with a pink crown on my head, fake earrings clipped on my ears, and getting a princess makeover.

I pull on some shorts, let out a yawn, and shuffle down the hallway to the kitchen. Tori hands me a mug of coffee that she took the liberty of adding cream to already. Even though I'm technically older, she joins my other sisters in feeling the need to take care of me. Even when puberty hit and I literally towered over all of them, their doting on me never faltered. You can pretty much guess how my mother treats me—that's where they all learned it from.

"Late shift last night?" She eyes me curiously while helping herself to a muffin from the box of freshly baked goodies my mom brought over yesterday.

"Yup, I worked the late shift—didn't get home till 2:30." I take a sip of my coffee. "That's why I was still sleeping when you so kindly woke me up."

She smiles, unfazed by my accusatory tone.

"Just helping you out. It's a beautiful day out there. Do you work tonight, too? I was thinking of going out."

"Yup, another late shift. I'll be there." I'm a lead bartender at The Toasted Crab, a bar in town right on the beach that overlooks the ocean. I've been adding extra shifts as much as I can lately. The owner, Mike, let us know last week that he'll be looking for a new bar manager within the next month, and dammit, I want that promotion. Bad.

Not that I dislike my role as bartender. I've just done it so long that I'm admittedly really good at it. Too good at it, maybe. Everything feels second nature to me, churning through the motions of each shift night after night. I can't help but be at a point where I'm a little bored with it all. I guess that's why I want this promotion so bad. I need more. More responsibility, more challenges, more decision-making opportunities. Just more.

I started working bartender shifts to make some extra cash when I was in college at the local university. By the time I graduated with a degree in business administration, I didn't really have a clear direction of what I wanted to do, and the tips I made from bartending were too good to let go.

So I started doing it full time, and here we are, a couple years later. I keep meaning to make a shift and actually use my degree, but there haven't been any opportunities that I've gotten excited about. I might as well try and move up the ladder as long as I'm still here.

"How's the love life? Any promising ladies?" she asks with a twinkle in her eye.

"You know I don't talk to any of you about girls. That's my one rule," I grumble.

As if summoned by the potential gossip, my door swings open without so much as a knock, and Emily comes strolling in. I never once gave any of them a set of keys to my apartment, but somehow, my mom and all four sisters wound up with their own copy. I suspect they somehow managed to convince my landlord to give them a set and then had copies made—one for each of them.

Traitor.

I roll my eyes, bringing my attention to the toast Tori slid in front of me.

"Hi!" Emily walks into the kitchen area. "What are you guys up to today?"

Like I do with most of our conversations, I wait for Tori to answer first. I find it's easier to let them get all of their talking out of their systems before trying to get a word in myself.

"I'm thinking of grabbing some lunch, then heading to the mall—do you want to come?" Tori asks Emily.

"Ooh, that sounds great! I need some new running gear, though. Can we hit the shoe store on the way, too?"

"Sure. Let's see if Grace and Ava want to join us." Tori pulls out her phone and starts typing.

"Oh, tell Ava that I have the dress I borrowed from her. It's in my car," Emily says, taking a bite of a chocolate-chip muffin.

Acknowledging that I'm not a part of this particular conversation, I make my way back to my room to take a quick shower before pulling on some khaki shorts and a white T-shirt. I run my fingers through my hair, slide my phone into my pocket, and grab my wallet.

"I'm out. See ya!" I call to my sisters, who grace me with side glances and quick waves, then I walk out the door and leave them to carry on without me.

I pour Casamigos into four shot glasses along the counter of the bar, then line them up in front of the women sitting at the bar in front of me, holding the gaze of the cute brunette for an extra beat.

"Four tequila shots. Enjoy, ladies!" I say with a wink, moving to the register at the end of the bar to enter in the last couple orders. It's been a relatively quiet evening, as most weeknights are. Granted, there's always a steady stream of tourists any day of the week, but the weekends are the busiest nights by far, always overflowing with a blur of people, barely allowing me to take a break. And although the weeknights could be deemed busy by any other standard, they feel slow in comparison to me.

Stacy, the other bartender working with me tonight, and I have easily got it handled. I grab a couple of empty glasses off the bar top, empty the ice and leftover lime wedges, then set them in the sink filled with soapy water next to me.

"Matty boy, how's it goin?" a familiar voice calls out from behind me.

A grin spreads across my face as I turn to find my longtime buddies, Brian and John, strolling toward the bar. In between them is John's girlfriend, Mia, looking stunning with her long blonde hair cascading over one shoulder.

"Hey! What's up?" I fist-bump Brian and John, then lean over the bar to give Mia a kiss on the cheek. She smiles at me sweetly, then slides onto the seat next to John, scooting it closer to him. He sits sideways, one leg on the back of her chair, caging her in, resting a hand on her thigh.

Seeing them together always makes me happy. John was in a rough spot last year, struggling with PTSD after coming home from a tour overseas with the Army. He was a broken man, and it tore me up inside to watch him suffer when there didn't seem to be a damn thing I could do to help him. Nothing I tried seemed to get through to him.

Along came Mia, and she slowly brought John back to life. For that alone, I will forever be grateful to her. Hibiscus Mai Tais for her for life as long as I'm around.

John, Brian, and I go way back. My family moved to Hawaii from Arizona in fourth grade, and the three of us became inseparable shortly after. We got into all kinds of trouble as kids —terrorizing the neighborhoods on our bikes, racing each other through town, and giving tourists the wrong directions. They're the brothers I never had.

"What can I get you guys?" I ask, setting three cocktail napkins down. They make their choices, and I chat with them as I get their drinks ready.

"So, when does Paige come in?" I ask, bracing myself for the eye rolls and jabs they'll inevitably shoot my way. They're always razzing me about having a thing for Paige. I don't deny it. There's something about that girl that captivates me and has from the very first time I laid eyes on her last year. She's not only incredibly stunning, but she's also snarky—which, apparently, I dig in a girl.

It's been a while since I've seen her in person, and it's not like I'm holding out hope for her—I've dated a few girls since the last time she was here—but she never really strayed too far from my mind. I've even sabotaged a few of her and Mia's FaceTime calls just to get a glimpse of her.

"Tomorrow!" Mia squeals. "I'm so excited!" Her eyes narrow as she leans forward. "You're gonna be on your best behavior, right?"

Now it's my turn to roll my eyes. I'm well aware of my reputation. I'm the resident flirt, hitting on women left and right. Do I flirt with pretty women often? Of course. I don't deny that. Do I enjoy the attention? Absolutely. But I'm not a womanizer by any means. I'm harmless. I just let accusations that I'm a ladies' man roll off my back. I can't change what other people think of me, and truthfully, I don't care enough to try.

"Mia, I'm a perfect gentleman. Can't you see that?"

John snorts next to her, then points down the bar. "Pretty sure I saw you flirting with that woman over there literally seconds before we sat down."

I follow his gaze just in time to catch the brunette eyeing me. She quickly looks away, a blush creeping over her cheeks. I'm well aware of my effect on women, and truthfully, I relish it. It gives me a rush when I know I'm the one getting them all flustered. I can't seem to help it.

I curl the corner of my mouth up into a smirk, push away from the bar, ignoring my friends, and turn to help a couple who just sat down.

I'm filling a glass with rum and Coke as Mike, the owner,

comes around the bar to check the beer inventory in the mini-fridge next to me.

"Matt, how's it going tonight?" he asks in a chipper voice.

"Great! Staying steady, no issues," I say with confidence.

"Perfect." He jots some numbers on the paper he's holding, then turns to walk in the opposite direction. "Keep up the good work, Matt. I've got my eye on you." He gives a small wave and heads back to his office. I smile smugly, hoping that fares well for me in the running for bar manager.

Brian, John, and Mia stay for another round and then leave, but not before I make them promise to not hide Paige from me all summer. I wave them off and spend the next few hours shuffling drinks around, clearing stations, and working my charm on the customers.

When 2:00 rolls around, I help close everything down and head back to my apartment. I find disassembled fajita ingredients that one of my sisters must have left me in the fridge, scarf it down, and head for bed. I strip down to my boxers and crawl into bed, exhausted, praying that I'll be able to sleep in tomorrow.

3

_____

PAIGE

I'm barely through the sliding doors at the airport when Mia comes barreling down the sidewalk, jumping on me with a squeal. I let out a squeal of my own, mine due to the fact that her momentum caused me to drop my bag, and we both tumble backward onto my suitcase. She lets out a laugh, which I follow with my own uncontrollable giggles.

I look up to see John rushing over to us, shaking his head at what must be a pathetic sight. He gently pulls Mia off, then offers his hand to me. When I'm finally upright, Mia wraps her arms around me in a tight hug.

"I missed you," she says quietly into my hair.

"I missed you, too," I whisper back with a smile. "I'm so excited to be in Hawaii again. I don't like being this far away from you!" I link my arm in hers, grab my carry-on bag, and follow John with my suitcase to his car.

On our way through town, Mia and I chat and catch each

other up on everything we missed in the last nine hours I've been traveling. She fills me in on her morning run and trip to Julie's Coffee and Juice Bar, and then I tell her about the lady next to me on the plane who fell asleep, and her head kept lolling to the side, hitting my shoulder. That was fun and awkward, trying to gently nudge her head upright with just enough finesse that she would stay vertical, and not too much where she'd be launched into the aisle.

I take in the palm-tree-lined streets and the swarm of people walking in swimsuits, cut-off shirts, and flip-flops. I inhale a deep breath. It's good to be back.

Before long, we're pulling into their driveway. A tiny twinge of envy sparks in my chest as I'm reminded, once again, that this beautiful house in paradise is where Mia calls home—complete with the love of her life, a pool, and an adorable cottage in the back. She's living the dream over here, and I'm so happy for her.

Hopping out, I grab my bag and reach for my suitcase. John beats me to it, ever the gentleman, and easily carries it inside. Mia links arms with mine and we head up the steps.

I've stayed in their cottage the last couple times I've visited, so this is the first time I'll be staying in the house with them. I know my way around by now, but as I follow Mia down the hall and into the guest room, I take in my surroundings.

To the left is a large dresser with a mirror centered above it, and there's a closet on the far wall. There's a queen-sized bed in the center of the room with a nightstand on one side that has a neatly wrapped gift package on top, which makes me smile. Mia always makes sure everyone around her feels spoiled and taken care of. I set my suitcase along the wall in the closet and throw my carry-on bag on top of the bed.

"I'll help you unpack later, if you want?" Mia asks from the doorway. "What do you want to do? Go to the beach? Go into town?"

I shrug, considering all of the options. "I'm not picky. How about the beach?"

"Good choice." She grins.

I change out of my comfy travel outfit and pull on a loose ivory tank top that I tuck into the front of my jean shorts. Grabbing my sunglasses, I meet Mia in the kitchen, where she's completely engulfed in John's arms.

If it weren't for her arms wrapping around his back, she would be nearly unnoticeable, her small frame almost entirely shielded by his muscles. Unfazed, I move around them to grab my phone out of my purse by the door. John clears his throat and stiffens when I enter his line of sight, but he still doesn't release his hold on her.

"Oh, don't mind me!" I tell him. "Honestly...don't change how you are with each other just because I'm here. You can suck her face all you want—I don't mind."

John gives me a tight smile while Mia laughs and plants a kiss on his cheek, untangling herself from his arms.

"We're gonna go to the beach for a bit. We'll be back in time to go to dinner. Love you."

John gives her a kiss on the lips. "Love you, too."

They're so adorable it's almost nauseating. I'm not cynical or anti-love, but it is hard to stop the envy that creeps up sometimes that I haven't been able to find my own happily ever after.

Don't get me wrong, I'm a confident, secure woman on my own, but that doesn't mean I don't hope for someone to share my life with. Someone to hold hands with when you're crossing the street, or to vent to after a long day, or even someone to think of when you see their favorite cookie at the grocery store. All of the mundane, day-to-day bits of life are so much more meaningful when you have someone you love to enhance them. It doesn't always feel fair that my perfect man hasn't come along yet when it seems like so many others are moving ahead with their lives at lightning speed.

It's definitely not from a lack of trying, either. I have so many cringey stories from my dating-app dates the last couple years to fill an entire book. There would be pages and pages detailing the nights I got stood up, the guys who wouldn't stop talking about themselves, and the ones who were too shy to even say a word. Granted, there have been some decent guys, just nobody I had a strong enough spark with to consider a second date.

It also doesn't help that I don't trust that easily. You can blame that one on my college boyfriend, Brandon, for dating me for two years only to abandon me for a scantily dressed cheetah at a *Wild in the Jungle* sorority party. Turned out, he'd been frequenting the safari our entire relationship.

Being cheated on and then enduring countless disappointing dates over and over again would make anyone hesitant to put themselves out there.

But, all of that considered, I'm still beyond happy for Mia and John. Their love is truly beautiful to watch, knowing how much they overcame to get here, and it gives me hope for my own true love someday.

Mia and I skip down the steps and make our way to the beach-access trail a little ways down the road. On the way, we stop to chat with a neighbor who's out for a walk, and then we wave to Rose, an elderly neighbor, as we pass by her house.

I marvel at Mia. She's always been a mostly happy person and makes friends wherever she goes, but there's something different about her here. There's an easiness about her. It's like she's lit up from the inside. A combination of pure joy and contentment radiates from her bones. It's something I've never seen before.

"I still can't believe this is your life. You're still happy, right?" I ask, already knowing the answer but fulfilling my best-friend duty by asking.

"I really am. I'm so stinking happy I have to pinch myself.

Honestly, Paige, between John and my job, it just almost seems like it's all too good to be true."

"You deserve to be happy, Mia." I loop my arm with hers and squeeze.

"Thanks, Paige." She smiles at me. "Should we be looking for a hot summer fling for you while you're here? I can ask around!"

A laugh bursts out. "I have a strict rule for myself to not be set up anymore, so no, thank you. Now, if it happens organically, then I'm all in. But I don't have the energy to force anything anymore."

We stop at the beach entrance and slide our shoes off, stepping onto the hot sand. We trudge along, slightly clumsily, through the sand until we reach the crystal-blue ocean. Letting it wash over our feet, a peace that I haven't felt in a while floods over me, and I'm giddy at the prospect of a stress-free summer here.

We find a spot on the sand and sit, spending the next hour chatting away about nothing and everything at the same time, as best friends do. A parasailing boat makes a few passes back and forth on the water, the parachute flying high above, legs dangling from the people brave enough to try it.

Eventually, we reluctantly brush the sand off of our bottoms and make our way back to get ready for dinner.

Back at the house, I change into a slate-gray romper and pull on some nude strappy sandals. As I'm sitting on the bed, having just finished fastening the straps on my shoes, I pick up the gift package from Mia and unpeel the cellophane wrapping.

Inside the basket is an assortment of travel-size toiletries—shampoo, conditioner, lotion, and after-sun cooling gel. The last item is a small, framed picture of Bradley Cooper, our shared celebrity crush ever since we binge-watched *The Hangover* movies in high school. I snort a laugh and set the frame upright on the nightstand, facing the bed. I won't mind his face being the last one I see every night before I fall asleep. Won't mind at all.

Across the hall in the bathroom, I fix my makeup that has almost completely melted off during my day of traveling and curl my shoulder-length hair. Mia joins me, and we finish primping, side by side, like we have a million times before, her shiny blonde contrasting with my dark, chocolatey brown hair. She applies some matte pinkish-nude lipstick, pops the cover back on, and then hands it to me. After we give each other nods of approval, we meet John in the kitchen.

"You both look stunning," John says as he plants a kiss on Mia's temple. "Brian wants to meet us at The Toasted Crab, but if you girls would rather go somewhere else, that's fine, too."

"Paige? It's your first night. You get to choose," Mia replies, setting her purse on the counter.

"The Toasted Crab's fine. I've been craving their grilled shrimp since the last time I was here," I reply, my stomach growling just thinking of it.

"You got it," John says. He holds the door and lets us pass him out into the garage, where we climb into his car. As we drive through town, I soak up all of the tropical vibes. The bright sunshine illuminates the sky, making the green of the palm trees pop and the flowers burst with color. As much as I love Minnesota in the summer, I can't say it has the same vivid backdrop as Hawaii.

When we arrive, we file in and make our way to the bar where Brian's waiting. He slides off his stool to greet us, giving me a hug and kiss on the cheek. I find a stool, climb on, and look up to see Matt behind the bar, his blue eyes smoldering directly into mine. His brows are furrowed together, creating a line that slides all the way up his forehead, stopping just under his short, dirty-blond hair. I can't get a read on the smolder—he's either liking the way I look tonight, or he didn't like the way that Brian greeted me.

I raise my eyebrows and flash him a smile. "Matthew," I say in greeting.

He seems to snap out of his trance, and he steps closer to us.

"Paige," he says, leaning across the bar, a husky mix of amusement and confidence laced in his voice. "You're looking exquisite as always. How was your flight?"

Before I can answer, Brian clears his throat. "Yo, man. What are we, chopped liver?"

Mia giggles and throws her arm around me, turning to Matt. "Easy there, Matt. She's only been here for, like, three hours. Let the girl breathe."

Matt grins and winks at me. "Can't help it," he says, his voice low and gravelly.

I can't help but smile. I have no interest in giving in to his incessant flirting, but that doesn't mean I don't acknowledge and appreciate the effort he puts in. What girl doesn't like being showered with praise? I can definitely enjoy the attention without getting sucked in.

He does look devilishly handsome in his black bartender uniform, though. I'll give him that.

After we place our drink orders, Mia turns to me. "Should we plan out everything we're going to do this summer while you're here? Obviously, I have to work during the day, but my evenings are all yours—sorry, John. Best friend trumps boyfriend when she's only here for two months."

John smiles and takes a sip of his beer. "Not a problem. I get it."

"I'm not gonna take you from John, Mia," I say with a laugh. "I'm a big girl. I can explore on my own when you guys want some alone time. And we can all hang out together, too."

"Does that include me?" Matt asks as he sets my margarita on a napkin in front of me.

I roll my eyes. "Sure, you can come, if that makes you happy."

He holds my gaze for a beat, then says in a low, slow voice, "Sure does."

Dang, he's good.

"You know, your charm doesn't work on me," I say in a direct, confident tone.

His eyes twinkle, seemingly finding amusement in the fact that I resist him. "Is that right?"

"Yup. Try all you want. I promise it won't work."

"That sounds like a challenge to me." Excitement flares in his eyes.

"Knock yourself out," I reply, refusing to let him have the last word.

He smirks, then backs away, holding eye contact until he eventually turns to tend to customers. I let out a breath that I wasn't aware I was holding. That whole interaction intrigues me. I might actually find enjoyment in messing with him while I'm here. You can tell he's used to women completely soaking up his attention and falling at his feet, but I won't be swayed by his admittedly gorgeous looks. I'm confident in that.

The rest of the evening passes quickly. Mia and I plan out a long list of adventures to go on while we eat our dinner, then we say bye to Matt and Brian and head back home.

I'm so exhausted from a long day of traveling that I hardly have the energy to wash my face or brush my teeth, but somehow, I manage to get all my bedtime routines finished. When my head hits the pillow, I whisper a quick goodnight to Bradley, then it doesn't take long to drift off to sleep.

4

MATT

"Hey, Ma!" I call out, pushing open my parents' front door and stepping inside. No one answers, so I make my way up the stairs into the kitchen, where I find my mom mixing some cookie batter in a bowl. She has earbuds in and is humming to herself while bobbing her head to music only she can hear.

Not wanting to scare her, I approach her from the side and gently lay a hand on her shoulder.

"Oh my!" she says after jumping in surprise. She brings a hand to her chest, the other one removing the earbuds. "You scared me!"

"Sorry, Ma. I yelled for you, but you didn't hear me. Having your own little rave party, huh?" I lean over and scoop some cookie dough out of the bowl with my finger, then retreat to a chair behind the counter before she slaps me with her spoon. She shoots me a stern look.

"Matthew...you do that again, and I'll use my spoon to

whoop you so hard your bottom will hurt for days," she says calmly, in a motherly tone she uses often and quite frankly scares me. I never know if she's kidding or not.

"Won't happen again. What do you have planned for today?" I ask as she sets a plate of already baked cookies in front of me. I have a great relationship with both my parents, but I've always been especially close to my mom. She always wanted to have a boy, and although she obviously loves my sisters, after having three girls, I was the answer to her prayers. I was the baby boy who could do no wrong, and boy did I milk that for all it was worth growing up.

When we moved here for my dad's job, my mom decided to retire from her own corporate job and stay at home to raise us. She really is the heart of our family. I credit the way she cultivated and nurtured our home life with how close we are as a family today.

She slides the next tray into the oven, then leans over the counter in front of me. "I'm meeting Ava and Lily at the park in an hour. You want to come?"

Lily is Ava and her husband, Steve's, two-year-old daughter. Ava is the only one of us who's married and has produced a grandchild, so behind me, she's currently Mom's second-favorite child.

"Nah, I'm gonna go meet up with John to surf for a little bit. Tell Lily that Uncle Matt will race her down the slide next time." That little girl has the whole family wrapped around her finger, myself included. There isn't a single thing I wouldn't do for her.

The front door opens, and Grace comes walking up the steps. My parents' house is a revolving door, the five of us constantly coming and going. My mom loves it and perpetuates that habit by keeping the fridge and pantry fully stocked and fresh-baked goods always on hand—the perfect environment to lure her adult children back home and keep her clued in on our lives.

Grace's eyes light up when she rounds the corner, and they land on me.

"Hey, Matthew! How's it going? How's work? You're staying out of trouble, right?" she teases, ruffling my hair. She pulls the milk out of the fridge, then pours two glasses, placing one in front of me as she takes a seat in the chair next to me. Everyone in my family calls me Matthew. To anyone else, I'm Matt—except for Paige, apparently, who called me by my full name last night. I didn't mind. It somehow sounded right when she said it.

Damn, was it good to see her. I knew I would be happy to see her, but I didn't anticipate the effect she had on me when I saw her walk through the door at the bar. I was frozen in place, my chest doing a weird tightening thing, and then I had to hold back the caveman impulse I had to knock Brian out when I saw him kiss her cheek. No clue where that came from. I've never been much of a jealous guy, but apparently, I might be when it comes to her.

"Always," I reply. "What's new with you? Jake still treating you with respect? I don't want to have to knock some sense into him, but I will." Jake is Grace's boyfriend, and even though I'm younger than him, I still take my role as brother seriously. I check in every once in a while just to make sure he knows my expectations. Tori and Emily aren't dating anyone seriously, so my protective-brother charm is all directed at Jake— unfortunately for him.

"The answer is still yes, just like it was two days ago when you asked." She rolls her eyes, tucking a strand of curly, dirty-blonde hair behind her ear, unaffected by my threats. If she thinks that'll stop me from keeping a tab on her dating life, she's sorely mistaken.

"Good. Make sure it stays that way." I push off the chair and give Mom a kiss on her cheek. "I'm off. See you guys later."

"Bye, Matthew. Don't forget to put sunscreen on," Mom

says, handing me a plate of cookies, and Grace waves goodbye with a smile.

I trudge slowly out of the water, carrying my surfboard under my arm, panting and legs aching after surfing for the past hour. John trails right behind me, and we both drop to the sand to catch our breath.

I'll never get sick of surfing. As exhausting as it is, it always invigorates and energizes me in a way that nothing else does. There's just something about feeling so in tune with the ocean while surfing. It's a connection, a give-and-take relationship with the ocean, where it feels like the wave is forming specifically for you. Riding the wave as it crests and breaks, then paddling out to do it all again, is like nothing else in the world. It feels like home out there to me.

We sit quietly on the sand for no less than two minutes when we hear Mia call out behind us.

"Looking good, boys!"

I twist my torso to see Mia and Paige sauntering toward us. That same weird tightening thing happens again in my chest when I focus on Paige. Her dark hair is pulled back in a bun, and she's wearing shorts and a black T-shirt.

Mia leans down to kiss John, then plops down next to him while Paige has a seat next to her.

"Did you just get here?" John asks them.

"About twenty minutes ago," Paige responds. "Couldn't miss the chance to see those big surfer muscles in action."

I mean, it's too easy. I can't help myself.

"Oh, you want to see them in action, huh? You should have told me. You won't believe what these muscles can do," I tease.

She rolls her eyes, seemingly regretting her choice of words. "Gross," she says with a laugh. "I have no interest in seeing what your muscles are capable of doing, thank you very much."

I chuckle, liking that she isn't one of those girls that gets easily offended by my personality and can actually dish it right back to me. Those kind of girls are hard to come by.

"Paige and I were thinking of walking to that tiki hut over there to grab some burritos for dinner. You guys want to come with?"

"Sure." The word flies out of my mouth before I even have a chance to wonder if I was included in Mia's invitation. John shoots me a sideways glance and turns back to Mia.

"Let's do it."

My Jeep is in a parking lot not too far away, so we go strap our surfboards to the top of my car before starting the walk down the beach. John crouches down and offers his back to Mia. She jumps on, wrapping her arms around his shoulders while Paige falls into step next to me.

"You know, I could offer you a ride if you wanted one, too, but you weren't interested in these muscles, so…" I shrug.

She smirks. "My legs are fully capable, thank you."

"Suit yourself."

We walk in comfortable silence, with John and Mia a little ways ahead of us. I hang back to walk with Paige, our feet falling into step next to one another, sinking further into the sand with each step.

"Do you work tonight?" she asks, peering over at me through her sunglasses.

"I do. Gotta head there in a little bit." I appreciate her attempt at small talk and figure I'll take this opportunity to get to know her a little bit more. She's made it clear that she's not interested in dating me, and I respect that—not that it'll stop me from flirting, of course—but that doesn't mean we can't be friends.

"You're a teacher, right?"

I wonder if she knows that her whole face lights up at the mention of her job. "Yup! Second grade."

"That must be exhausting," I muse. "Don't get me wrong, I love kids… But man, teachers are saints. God knows I definitely gave my teachers a run for their money."

She snorts. "I don't even want to know what kind of student you were, but yes, it can be exhausting. It's also extremely rewarding, though." She glances over at the ocean. "Being the person responsible for those lightbulb moments when they finally learn something new is unlike anything else."

I nod, recalling similar situations with Lily.

"Do you like being a bartender?"

"I do. The social piece, building relationships and interacting with people every night never gets old, but I also really enjoy the whole process—making and serving drinks, completing transactions, clearing dishes, making sure everything is fully stocked—and doing it all as efficiently as possible. It's a rush. I get a high from staying on top of everything." It's technically not a lie. I really do enjoy all those parts of my job. I just left out the part where I used to feel it a little stronger than I do now, that it feels like something's missing.

"That's awesome. I thought you just liked standing there looking pretty for all the girls to ogle at."

"Well, that's just a given. The girls ogle everywhere I go, but I'm flattered that you think I'm pretty." I wink at her.

She rolls her eyes again, and I wonder how many times in one day I could make her roll her eyes. I have a feeling that number would be high.

"There's an opening for a management position." I can't seem to help opening up a little more. "I've been picking up as many shifts as possible to try and get the job. I'd love to be part of the back end of running a bar a little more, you know?"

"Good for you." Paige glances up, and her eyes hold mine for a moment as if she's studying me, her expression unreadable.

I can't bring myself to look away, so I hold her gaze, and something in her green eyes makes my heart start beating just a touch faster. Then, she looks down at the sand with a smirk. "Look at that. You really are capable of having a conversation without flirting."

I shrug. "You should hear what's going on in my head, though," I say with a smirk.

She lets out a laugh just as Mia hops off of John's back, returning to Paige's side.

"What are you in the mood for, Paige? Chicken or beef burrito?" They loop their arms around each other, then venture off to the tiki hut.

The quick backward glance Paige gives me has me thinking that I will undoubtedly take anything I can get with this woman —even if she only wants to be friends.

5

PAIGE

"Make sure you give Harley his pain pills every night before bed, okay? Otherwise, he'll be up all night, pacing," I remind my mom through the phone. I called to check in, technically on everybody back home, but mostly on Harley.

Harley is our ten-year-old black lab. My parents surprised my brother, Caleb, and me with him when he was a puppy. He's been my little sidekick ever since. I was heartbroken to be away from him when I left home for college, and the second I found my own apartment that allowed dogs, I begged my parents to let me take him. They, of course, were attached, too, so Harley has been splitting his time 50/50 between their house and mine.

He's getting up there in age. The pain pills are for the arthritis in his hips that makes walking up the stairs a struggle for him. I dropped him off a few days before I came here, and I miss him terribly already.

"I know, dear. He's my dog, too, remember?" She laughs.

"He definitely misses you, though. How are things going there? All settled?"

"Everything's great so far! It's really nice to be back, and I'm mostly settled." I eye my suitcase in the corner that I have yet to unpack. I've been here for a few days now, but Mia and I have been so busy that I've hardly had a chance to go through it. We've been off gallivanting around the island. Beach hopping and going on quests to find the best piña colada has been keeping us busy.

Today would have been a great day to unpack since she was working all day, but the pull of the ocean was stronger than the one to unpack, so I ended up lounging on the beach most of the day.

Mia is a contributor for the local newspaper in Honolulu. She writes her own column—a travel guide of sorts. She highlights tourist attractions and hidden gems that she's discovered. I'm happy for her that she found a job she loves, one that allows her to explore and connect with locals. I'm excited to tag along on some of her adventures while I'm here, but today, she was interviewing the owner of a new ice cream shop in town, so I opted to stay and keep avoiding my suitcase.

"How are Dad and Caleb?" I ask Mom. My brother, Caleb, is younger than me. He just finished his first year of college at St. John's University in Collegeville. We have a pretty close relationship, as most siblings do when they grow up moving from one military base to another. Our father was a pilot in the Air Force, so we moved around quite a bit until he retired when I was in eighth grade, and we settled down in Minnesota. Caleb was in second grade at the time, and I'm glad he had a little bit more stability than I did growing up. The constant moving made it hard to build and maintain friendships. Karma made up for that, though, by eventually giving me the best friend a girl could have in Mia.

"They're both doing great! Caleb found an apartment near

campus with some friends, so he'll be moving in there next week. Lord help his neighbors. They're a rowdy bunch," she says with a laugh. "We sure are going to miss you this summer. Who am I going to go to brunch with?"

"I'm sure you'll be fine, Mom. And I'll be back before you know it," I say, chuckling, as I hear the front door closing.

"Mom, Mia's back. I gotta go. Give Harley a big squeeze for me, please. Love you."

I hang up and move down the hall to the kitchen, where Mia is just setting her laptop bag on the counter.

"Hi! How was your day?" she asks with a smile while sliding onto a barstool and pulling her laptop out. "I just need to jot a few things down while they're fresh in my mind, if you don't mind, then I'm all yours!"

"Take your time," I reply, sliding onto the stool next to hers, content to sit quietly while she finishes her work. I grab my phone and aimlessly scroll through my social media.

John opens the door and strolls in, running his hand through his wet hair.

"Hi, babe. How was your surfing lesson?" Mia asks, still typing away furiously.

John plants a kiss on her temple, his hand grazing between her shoulder blades. "It was great. Aiden finally got up and rode a wave, so it was a big day. I'm gonna go shower quick. Be right back." She nods in response, and John heads down the hallway.

I head to the fridge to grab something to drink when the door flies open again, and my head instantly swings to the left.

"Quinn!" Mia shrieks in surprise, jumping off her stool to give her a hug. My jaw drops open as John's sister sets down her luggage and wraps her arms around Mia.

"What are you doing here? I thought you weren't coming home until Thanksgiving?"

Quinn lifts her arms wide and shrugs. "I changed my mind.

I'm officially done with Alaska. It's not the state for me. I'm moving home for a while!"

I don't know Quinn well, but given what I do know of her, this isn't all that surprising. I recall past conversations where Mia alluded to the fact that she was impulsive, so this behavior fits, but I'm still a little bewildered that she's actually here.

"Oh my gosh!" Mia squeals, gesturing to me. "Quinn, you remember my best friend, Paige? You've met on FaceTime before, right?"

Quinn looks over at me with a friendly smile. "Yes! It's so nice to meet you in person. Any friend of Mia's is a friend of mine."

"Quinn? What the hell are you doing here?" John comes into view from the hallway, still pulling his shirt over his head. Quinn rushes toward him and wraps John in an embrace. He squeezes her tight in return, and I smile at the affection between the two of them. They lost both their parents years ago, and from what I've heard, they drifted apart when they were working through their grief. Then, they went through another rough patch when John was struggling last year. It's heartwarming to see them together. Mia's mentioned how close they are now.

"She's here to stay! Isn't that great?" Mia asks, jumping up and down in excitement.

"Seriously?" John asks, releasing Quinn.

"Yup!" She looks at me. "But don't worry, Paige, I knew you were staying here this summer, so I'm planning to stay with some friends until I can find my own place."

Guilt creeps into my chest, and after a mere moment, I make a decision that ultimately was not hard to make at all.

"Oh no...you know what? You should stay here with Mia and John. I'll go stay at a hotel. Honestly, it's no problem at all!"

"No, I couldn't ask you to do that, Paige! I wasn't expecting to stay here, seriously!"

Mia looks between the two of us, her face wrecked with the conflicted emotions she's clearly feeling.

"No, seriously. I don't mind at all! I haven't even unpacked my suitcase yet, so it's not a big deal!" I can feel Mia's guilty eyes burning into me. "Honestly, Mia. I'll be fine. She's family. She deserves to stay here with you guys."

She opens and then shuts her mouth, struggling to find the right words. "But I invited you to stay here. How about I come stay at the hotel with you?"

"No, that's ridiculous. Stay here with John and Quinn. I'll still see you every single day. Promise."

"You're absolutely sure about this?" Quinn asks guiltily. "I really don't mean to put you out."

"Yup! Absolutely. I'm glad you're here," I say with a smile.

"We don't have tenants coming to stay in the cottage for a couple more days. Why don't you stay there, for now, Quinn, while we work everything out?" John suggests.

"Great idea!" Mia replies, clapping her hands together, then letting out a shriek. "Eek! How about a celebratory cocktail to celebrate all three of my favorite people here in one place?"

"Yes!" I say with a grin, trying to convey how truly okay I am with the situation. I wouldn't be able to live with myself if I didn't offer up my guest room to Quinn, who belongs here with them more than I do.

I help Mia whip up some blended margaritas while Quinn fills us in on life in Alaska. She alludes to the fact that she broke things off with a boyfriend before coming home, but she won't give us any more detail than that. We can all empathize with the long, cold winters, and we cheers to being in this warm, tropical climate with no snow in sight.

"Why don't you bring your drinks outside?" John asks. "I'll grill us some burgers."

"Great idea, babe," Mia says.

We carry our drinks and the pitcher out into the sun, letting our feet dangle by the side of the pool.

I always knew I would get along with Quinn, but I didn't realize just how much I would like her. She reminds me of myself and Mia—outgoing, girly-girl, adventurous. I know we'll get along great, and I think John knows it, too, judging by the countless times he sighs and shakes his head.

"I'll make a salad to go with the burgers," Mia says, standing up. Quinn and I follow her inside to help, and we eventually bring it out to a table where John placed the burgers.

The rest of the evening is spent laughing, chatting, and enjoying the humid Hawaiian air that envelops each of us. It's absolutely perfect, and when my head hits the pillow that night, even though my rooming situation is still up in the air, I find myself feeling extremely grateful.

6

MATT

"What'd I do this time? It must be serious if you're both here."

John and Mia are standing in my doorway, their eyes throwing daggers into mine as I stand here, holding open the door, trying to figure out what I need to apologize for this time. I wish I could say it wasn't a common occurrence for me to inadvertently offend someone, but I admit it happens occasionally.

"We need to talk to you," John says, moving past me to sit on the couch. Mia follows and sits next to him, clasping her hands together and looking up at me expectantly. It reminds me of how my mother always looks at me when she's about to scold me for whatever childish antics I'd gotten into that day.

I take a deep breath and sit on the chair to the right of the couch, leaning forward toward them, bracing myself for whatever they're about to say.

"Alright, give it to me."

Mia clears her throat. "Well, here's the thing. Did John tell you Quinn's back in town?"

"Uh-huh," I say slowly, wondering where this is going.

"She's moving home, which is amazing! The problem is, the cottage is all booked up, and we only have one guest room. Paige kindly offered to stay in a hotel for the rest of her stay so Quinn can stay with us, which was super gracious of her, and I love her for it, but I'm being selfish and don't want to have her so far away. The closest hotel is all the way in town."

The side of my mouth slowly turns up into a smug grin, understanding where this conversation is heading.

"Sooo, you're here to ask for my help? To see if she can stay in my guest room?"

John nods. "Yes, if that's alright with you, of course."

Mia jumps in, "We haven't asked Paige yet, so obviously, it's up to her, but we wanted to come talk to you first and make sure you are alright with a few things before we talk to her." She clears her throat and shifts slightly forward. "Ready?"

I nod my head in amusement.

"First, if she agrees to stay here, if she feels uncomfortable at any second, I will have John beat you to a pulp, understand?" She pauses for effect, staring me down, but my expression doesn't change. "Second, you will treat my best friend with respect. Keep your dirty little hands off of her while she's staying here, okay?"

My eyes narrow. "Did you come here to insult me or ask for my help?"

"Ask for your help, obviously, but what kind of best friend would I be if I didn't protect her?"

"Well...I'm offended that you think she needs protecting from me, but sure, if she wants to stay here, the room's all hers." I can't help but be intrigued at the prospect of her living here with me. Not that I think anything would happen. And obviously, I wouldn't try—I know where she stands. But I definitely like the fact that I would be able to see her more often.

Mia eyes me skeptically, pushing her lips together. "Okay. 'Cause you know I'm pretty scrappy, too. I'll totally throw down for Paige if I need to."

John and I chuckle while he places a calming hand on her thigh. "I think he gets it, Mia."

She nods her head in contentment. "Okay, as long as we're on the same page." She relaxes into the couch, shedding her comical tough exterior that she tried so hard to portray. "Like I said, we haven't suggested this to her as an option yet, but we'll talk to her today and see what she thinks. I would love having her right here—only a mile away—versus trekking all the way to the hotel to see her."

"Just let me know what she says," I say to her, then turn to John. "You up for surfing today?"

"I'm teaching a lesson at eleven. You wanna meet me after that?"

"Yup," I say, rising from the chair. "I'd love to be a polite host and offer you something to drink, but apparently, I'm a terrible person to be around," I tease. "And I need to shower, anyway."

Mia rolls her eyes. "There's no way I hurt your feelings. You're the most conceited person I know. You'll be just fine."

"Ouch," I reply, clutching my hand to my chest to feign being insulted. "Now you really did it. Out you go." I open the door and usher them both out of my apartment. Once the door is closed, I shake my head in amusement and head to shower for the day.

"I think that's the last of it," John says later that evening as he sets Paige's suitcase in my entryway, next to a few more of her bags and some groceries. Mia and Paige are in the kitchen, opening cabinet doors, inspecting the food I have in the fridge.

It's a good thing I'm used to having my space invaded, otherwise, this would be a pretty annoying start to our roommate situation. Besides, I'm pumped that Paige agreed to move in here. I have a feeling nothing could bring my mood down.

"Why do you have food in here with your name on a Post-it note?" Mia giggles, rotating a takeout container in her hand. My mom orders those things in bulk online every year. Evidently, they're perfect for feeding your only son and contributing to the family hobby of babying him.

"That would be either my sisters or my mom. They like to make sure I'm well fed," I tell them matter-of-factly.

"Oh Lord, you're not one of those guys who's incapable of taking care of himself, are you?" Paige asks.

"I can take care of myself just fine," I say, grabbing the milk container from under Mia's nose, placing it back inside, and shutting the fridge door. "There's no stopping them. Believe me, I've tried."

Mia shrugs. "Okay, well, we're heading into town for dinner. You sure you don't want to come with us?" she asks Paige.

"No, I'm gonna get unpacked and settled. Have fun, though! I'll meet up with you tomorrow."

Mia and John head out the door but not before Mia throws me one last warning glare, which I respond to with a smug grin and a wave.

"So, Matthew… " There she goes saying my full name again. I glance over to see her tucked behind the kitchen counter, her eyes meeting mine. My breath gets caught in my throat. There's something about her deep, emerald-green eyes that pulls me in. I can't seem to look away. Her eyes stay locked with mine for a beat until, eventually, she blinks and clears her throat.

"First of all, thank you for letting me stay here. I admit, this is a much better option than staying at a hotel. Second, just because I agreed to stay here, that doesn't mean I don't have some ground rules."

I nod, striding across the room to rest my arms on the counter, leaning closer to her, her eyes still following mine.

"Let's hear 'em."

"Okay, I'm a little bit particular about my food. Is it reasonable enough to assume that the food I get for myself will not be touched or eaten by you?"

"That surprises me. I pegged you to be generous, teaching kids how to share and all that."

"Yeah, well, not when it's my own food, unfortunately. Sorry, I know it's kind of diva-ish, but it's just the way I am. Besides, it looks like your family keeps you well stocked with food, so that shouldn't be a problem."

"Shouldn't be an issue," I agree. "What else you got?"

"Can I ask that you give me a warning when you bring your lady friends over? I prefer to not be woken up by you bringing a girl back here—especially if my room is right across the hall, if you know what I mean."

"Paige, I'm offended. You're the only one I've got eyes for. You know that," I tease.

She rolls her eyes. "Yeah, right. I know how you operate."

"Be considerate when it comes to other chicks—got it." She doesn't realize how easy that one'll be. I don't foresee myself bringing any girls back here, especially when I know Paige will be in the next room.

"That's it," she says with a genuine smile, her eyes distracting me again. "I really am appreciative of you letting me stay here. I'm a good roomie, I promise. Wanna give me the tour?"

"Sure thing," I say, drumming my hands on the counter. "Well, you've already seen the kitchen, and right across there is the living room. That's my favorite chair next to the couch. It's literally impossible for me to play Grand Theft Auto unless I'm in that chair." I pause to let the seriousness of the situation sink in.

"No sitting in your special chair. Noted." She pushes her lips together like she's either trying not to laugh at me, or she's irritated with me—honestly could be either.

"K, moving on." I motion for her to follow me down the hallway. "On your left is the bathroom we'll be sharing. Sorry—it's only a one-bathroom unit—I'm working with a bartender salary over here. But I promise I'm not gross. I learned early on to keep my disgusting boy side under wraps around women, so that'll work in your favor.

"And then, on the right is my room." I push the door open wide enough to give her a glimpse inside, then pause. "I hope you know it's taking everything in me to not crack a joke about inviting you inside my bedroom, but you know, I'm a gentleman, what can I say…" Paige rolls her eyes and smirks. That's two tallies for an eye roll. I'm sure there are many more to come.

I lead her a few more steps down the hallway, where her room is on the left. "This lovely room will be all yours. Scout's honor to not invade your space—unless you invite me in, of course," I say with a smirk, which apparently has no effect on her whatsoever because she completely ignores me.

"Alright, let me help you with your bags, and then you can get situated."

"What are you gonna do? Go sit in your special chair?"

"Don't worry about it," I reply.

I grab her suitcase while she carries her smaller bags down to her room. Leaving her suitcase next to her bed, I head back to the living room to watch some TV while she gets settled. I sit in my chair and flip through the channels, the whole time acutely aware that Paige is in my apartment and wondering what she's doing back there.

I'm not sure how I'll be able to focus on anything other than her while she's here. It's a constant nagging thought in the back of my mind that refuses to go away.

Is she unpacking?

Does she want company?

Maybe I should go check on her.

No.

Don't be weird.

After a little while, Paige puts me out of my misery and comes strolling into the kitchen. She grabs two bottles of Gold Cliff IPA from the fridge and hands me one as she passes by to sit on the couch.

I open mine in amusement. "I thought you didn't share your stuff."

"I don't usually. Consider it a token of my appreciation for letting me stay here. Just don't expect it to happen again."

"Noted." I nod. We spend the next hour mindlessly watching TV until she climbs off the couch.

"I'm off to bed. Night, Matt," she says casually, already making her way down the hall. I stare after her, my tongue caught in my throat for some reason. Eventually, I snap out of it right before she goes into her room.

"Night, Paige."

7

PAIGE

I shuffle down the hallway the next morning in my pajama shorts and tank top in search of coffee. My head is still fuzzy from sleep, lingering grogginess from the jet lag only adding to my typical morning fog. I bring my hand up to cover my yawn, zeroing in on the Keurig next to the fridge, and push my glasses up higher on the bridge of my nose.

I can't even get dressed without my first caffeine fix of the day, let alone trust myself to put my contacts in yet. I place a coffee pod in the machine and press start, then glance at the clock on the stove and see that it's 9:18 a.m. I haven't slept in this late since last summer, and I fully intend on taking advantage of my schedule-free days while I'm here. So far, mission accomplished.

When Mia told me that Matt had offered up his guest room for me to stay in, I'll admit—as insufferable as he is—I was excited at the thought. I'm comfortable enough with him that staying here wouldn't be awkward, and it definitely is closer to Mia. It'll be so much easier to meet up from here. Not to mention the fact that I don't have a copious amount of funds to spend on staying at a hotel for the rest of the summer, and that would have totally drained my bank account. It was an easy yes for me.

"Has anyone ever told you that you look like a freaking goddess in the morning?"

I snort into my coffee cup that was just about to touch my lips, surprised at Matt's voice behind me. I turn to face him head-on, bringing my still puffy eyes up to meet his.

"Ha, yeah, I'm sure I'm wildly attractive right now," I retort. "This isn't going to help your crush on me, you know."

Matt nods his head in sincere agreement. He's wearing no shirt and a pair of gray sweatpants that sit low on his hips. I force my eyes away from his muscular chest to focus on my coffee as I take a sip. He moves behind me to grab a mug of his own out of the cupboard, and when he turns around, his eyes give me a slow scan.

"You got that right. The glasses…the disheveled Medusa hair…the whole look. I'm digging it." He nods absent-mindedly, like he just confirmed the thought to himself. The smallest flutter of butterflies starts dancing in my stomach before I quickly remind myself, once again, that he's just a flirt. He does this with all women.

I laugh. "Sorry, still not affected by your charm. Friends, remember? And if this look works for you, I'm sorry to warn you that you'll have to get used to it. This particular form of torture will be here every single morning."

He sighs, shaking his head, bringing half of his mouth up into a smirk. "I'll gladly endure that torture."

I roll my eyes and step next to him to grab an apple from the fruit basket I brought yesterday, then walk around to have a seat on a barstool that's settled under the counter that overlooks the kitchen. I take another sip of coffee, feeling the caffeine slowly breathe new life into me.

"What do you have planned for today?" Matt asks, leaning his hip against the counter, sipping his coffee. I'm momentarily distracted by the broad muscles of his chest and shoulders. I snap my eyes back up before they trail to his stomach.

I shrug, ignoring the smug look on his face. "I'm not sure. I'm actually surprised Mia hasn't called yet, her being in protective mama-bear mode and all."

He chuckles, his eyes yet to stray from me.

"What about you?" I ask.

"I have to work, but not till later tonight. Oh, by the way, just a heads up—when I work the late shift, I won't be getting home till 2:30ish. I'll be quiet, so I don't wake you. Just thought you should know. Don't wanna freak you out."

"Got it. If I hear noises in the middle of the night, I won't attack you with a baseball bat."

"Unless you're into that kinda thing." He smirks. He must pick up on the lack of amusement on my face. He shrugs his shoulders, unaffected.

My phone chirps with a text-message notification from down the hall in my room. I slide off the stool, place my mug in the dishwasher, and start heading for my room.

"I'm gonna go shower. See ya in a bit," I say over my shoulder to Matt, not bothering to turn around but feeling his eyes on me the whole way down the hall.

I grab my phone off the nightstand and see that Mia had sent a message to a group text chain that includes myself, John, Matt, and Brian.

Mia: Beach volleyball, anyone?

I'm just about to type out a response when I hear Matt call

out from his room, "I hope you're ready to get your butt kicked. I'm a master at beach volleyball!"

"Well, prepare for a challenge. My team won first place in a four-state tournament," I yell back. He doesn't need to know that it was a junior tournament when I was ten, and I haven't played since. I can't resist the urge to challenge his ego a little bit. It's far too tempting.

"Game on, Medusa."

∼

"How was your first night at Matt's?" Mia asks me as we drink some water and get ready to start playing. We're both wearing sports bras and running shorts. I had a tank top on as well, but that quickly came off after two minutes of being in this sweltering heat. The mid-day Hawaiian sun is no joke.

"It was good! Got a good night's rest. Matt's tolerable so far. How are things going with Quinn?"

"Great! It's so nice having her here. We invited her to play today, too, but she's catching up with some friends instead."

"I'm glad it's going well." I smile at her while pulling my hair up into a bun. I glance over to where John and Matt are tossing the volleyball back and forth. Brian's nearby, taking a swig of his water, chatting with his buddy, Eric, who he invited so we could play three-on-three. The boys already worked out the teams. Apparently, there's some kind of intricate strategy when it comes to choosing teams, taking weight, athletic build, and competitiveness into consideration. Mia, John, and Matt will be on one team, while Eric, Brian, and I are on the other.

"Ready, ladies?" John calls, walking to one side of the net.

"Good luck!" Mia gives me a smile and a high-five, and she runs off to join him. I join Brian and Eric on the court.

"Alright, let's have some fun!" Brian says as he grabs the ball and takes the serving position. I walk to the left side of the net while Eric takes the right. Somehow, I'm not surprised when Matt takes the position directly across from me on the other side of the net. He crouches down, places his hands on his thighs, his eyes roaming over every inch of me.

"Eyes up here, Romeo." I wave two fingers in front of my eyes, encouraging his gaze to raise at least a few inches. I don't get a creepy vibe from Matt at all—he amuses me more than anything—so I chuckle when his eyes reluctantly rise to meet mine, and I hold his gaze as Brian serves the ball over the net, hitting the sand right next to Matt with a thud.

"Matt! What the hell?" John calls, breaking him out of his trance.

I laugh. "Is this all it's gonna take to beat you? This is gonna be easier than I thought."

He shakes his head, determination washing over his face, then he motions for John to switch positions with him. Stretching his arms out in front of him, he cranes his neck from side to side and then glances over to shoot me a wink.

I can't help but let out a laugh in amusement.

"Okay, are we ready now?" Brian asks.

"Yes. Let's go!" I reply, shifting my feet in the sand and clapping my hands together.

He sends another serve effortlessly over the net, which John bumps right back, the ball coming in my direction. I send up a quick prayer to the volleyball gods and make contact with the ball, setting it for Eric to spike over the net, earning us a point.

"Oh my gosh! Good job, Paige!" Mia shouts in excitement.

"Mia, she's on the other team," Matt grumbles.

"What about me?" asks Eric.

I just laugh and get ready for the next play. For the next hour, we play a surprisingly close game of beach volleyball. We win, admittedly mostly thanks to Brian and Eric, but that won't stop me from relishing in the bragging rights. I only tease Mia and Matt a couple times before we all jump in the ocean, letting the water cool our bodies. The waves splash onto the backs of my legs as I make my way out onto the sand, grabbing for a towel to dry off.

"You guys want to hit up Marty's?" John asks the group. Everyone agrees, and after walking down the beach a little way, I see a sign that says Marty's Beach Bar fastened to the top of an older building. It sits right on the edge of the sand with a sidewalk on the side leading all the way out to the main road. The exterior is made up of faded red wood, and three steps with a white railing lead up to a white door with two windows on either side. Palm trees flank each side of the bar.

Matt holds the door open for all of us, making eye contact with me as I pass by. Something prompts me to take a reprieve from my teasing, and I give him a genuine smile instead, which he sends right back to me in return. Apparently, my Matt armor isn't completely shatter-proof, because my heart skips a beat.

Mentally shaking it off, I follow Brian to a high-top table just a few steps to the right. Sliding onto a stool, I glance around. It's definitely an older establishment, with paint wearing off the walls, and a few cracks in the floorboards. A couple of fans are swirling lazily above us. There are a few groups of people scattered at different tables, and an older gentleman is behind the bar, mixing a drink.

"Is that Marty?" I ask Matt, who's sliding onto the stool next to me.

"Yup. Solid guy. We've known him for years."

"He's the sweetest guy," Mia chimes in. "Poor thing lost his wife a few years ago. I'm sure if you get him talking, he'll tell you a story or two about her."

Marty drops off a couple beers at a table nearby, then turns to us with a smile. "Well, if it isn't my favorite bunch of troublemakers," he says, patting John on the back. Then, he turns to Mia and me. "Mia, hello. You two look like sweet girls. What in the world are you doing with these fellas? They tell you about all the mischief they got into as young gentlemen?" He chuckles, shaking his head.

"Hey, now. We weren't that bad," John says, a touch of guilt flashing on his face.

"What can I get ya?" Marty asks, laughing him off.

We place our orders—strawberry daiquiris for Mia and me and beers for John, Brian, and Eric. Matt orders a water since he'll be working in a few hours. Marty nods and disappears behind the bar.

Eric clears his throat next to John. "So, Paige, how long you in Hawaii for—"

"Nope," Matt immediately barks out. "No. Sorry, buddy, but it ain't gonna happen. She's off limits."

Mia stifles a giggle while I'm momentarily stunned by his boldness.

"Excuse me?" I ask in amusement.

Matt shrugs innocently. "Sorry. You want to date, go ahead, but not while I'm here. I can't watch. Can't do it."

I laugh at the absurdity of it all. "Oh my goodness, you are something else."

Eric laughs, raising both hands in the air. "Sorry, didn't mean to overstep."

"You're fine," I reassure Eric, then I turn to Matt. "Um, just so we're on the same page here, you don't get to dictate who I talk to. Got it?"

Matt's crystal-blue eyes hold mine for a beat, his mouth eventually turning up into a smirk. He absentmindedly scratches along the line of his jaw and then nods his head in defeat. "My apologies. Won't happen again."

"Good," I say with satisfaction, turning to my right to change the subject. I've had enough overt displays of masculinity for one day. "Mia, tell me more about that couple you interviewed this morning for work."

Mia fills me in on the latest article she's working on, and we chit chat for a few minutes—all while trying to ignore my heartbeat, that I'm all of a sudden more aware of after Matt's outburst—until Marty sets our daiquiris in front of us.

The pinkish-red icy drink is a welcome distraction and looks especially appealing after a few hours in the hot sun. I take the paper umbrella off the top and lift it up.

"To the best summer ever," Mia says, raising her own glass.

I clink my drink with hers. "Cheers."

8

MATT

"Do you ever put a shirt on?"

I lift my coffee, eyebrows raised, and turn to see Paige shuffling into the kitchen, reaching for the fridge door.

"Is that disgust I hear in your voice?" I scoff. "Yeah, see, that's how I know you're full of it. Nobody's repulsed by these abs."

I'm really not this conceited—okay, maybe I am a little bit—but I like to play up the whole self-absorbed act for effect. I like seeing what kind of reaction I can get from women. Harmless fun, if you will, and it seems to come out in spades around Paige.

She huffs. "I'm not awake enough to bring your ego back down to earth. Will you just do it for me?"

I smirk, taking in the sight of her. Her eyes are still half closed behind her glasses. She's wearing a tight gray tank top and black cotton shorts. The unruly, tangled mess of dark hair on her head is the perfect complement to her scowl. The corner of my mouth lifts up in a smirk.

Morning Paige might just be my favorite.

I slide the mug of coffee I brewed for her down the counter in her direction. She looks at the coffee, then back at me with caution—like she's trying to figure out if I spit in it or not.

"You made me coffee?" The skepticism in her eyes softens a bit as she takes a sip.

I shrug. "No big deal. I knew you were up. I heard you moving around in your room, and I was already in the kitchen." I busy myself with placing dishes into the dishwasher, trying to gloss over the nice gesture I just made. If I look her in the eyes right now, I might just blurt out what I haven't been able to get my own head around yet—that she's been invading every square inch of my brain. Every single thing I do, I find myself thinking about her.

What kind of toothpaste does she prefer? What flavor Chapstick does she use? Does she wear socks with her slippers? What's her go-to Starbucks order? I haven't been able to think of anything else but her since the second she moved in, but she doesn't need to know that. I've gotta figure out a way to snap out of this consuming crush I have on her, 'cause it's getting ridiculous.

"I didn't put any creamer or anything in it yet. Figured you'd wanna do that part," I tell her.

"Thank you," she says as she takes a seat on a stool. "Is this an apology for yesterday with Eric? For marking your territory like some alpha male?" Her brows lift up, green eyes burning into mine, hints of both accusation and amusement in them.

I smile sheepishly, leaning my hip against the counter. "Yeah, I guess I do owe you an apology for that." My apology is cut short by the sound of the front door swinging open.

"Help, please!" Tori calls from behind the tall stack of boxes she's carrying. I grab the stack and bring them back to the kitchen, catching Paige's wide and confused eyes that are pinned on Tori.

Shit.

I haven't had a chance to tell my family about Paige moving in yet, because the longer I could spare her from dealing with my sisters, the better. I also haven't told Paige about my overbearing family yet. I open my mouth to introduce them when Tori spots Paige, stops in her tracks, and gasps.

"Oh my gosh, do I actually get to meet one of Matthew's girlfriends?" she squeals. "He usually keeps them far away from us. Eek! I'm Tori, Matt's sister. It's so nice to meet you!" She doesn't wait for a response before rambling on.

"Okay, forewarning, we like to tease him a little bit—okay, a lot—and we kind of baby him sometimes. That tends to bother his girlfriends—the few that he's allowed us to meet, anyway—so it's probably best I start with that to get it out of the way." She rushes over to Paige and engulfs her in a big hug. Paige awkwardly returns the hug, then clears her throat.

"Um…it's really nice to meet you, Tori. And believe me, I will gladly join you in making fun of Matt, but, uh…I'm not his girlfriend. I'm Paige, Matt's friend. He's nice enough to let me stay in his spare room for a few weeks while I'm here on vacation."

"Oh!" The expression on Tori's face morphs from disappointment to confusion to acceptance in a span of two seconds.

"Paige is Mia's best friend. She's here for the summer, and with Quinn coming home, she needed a place to stay," I say casually, mentally willing Tori to play it cool. Nobody escapes the interrogations of my sisters easily.

"Okay! Well, it's nice to meet you, Paige! So you're living in the guest room, huh? And one bathroom, phew. Has he been keeping things clean for you? We tried our best to train him to be an exceptional person to live with, but he is a guy, after all. There's only so much we could do."

"For the most part, yes. Although, I've only been here for a couple days. I'm sure I'll be sufficiently grossed out by the time I move out."

"No doubt," Tori replies, sliding onto the stool next to Paige.

I let out a sigh. "What's in the boxes?" I ask, attempting to change the subject. I peer in the top box to find an assortment of cookies.

"Mom and Lily had a baking day yesterday. The top box is cookies. The middle box is two different kinds of bread—banana and lemon-poppyseed. Then, the bottom box is an apple pie. Don't ask me how they had time to make so much. I have a whole set of boxes, too. It must have taken them all day. Help yourself, too, Paige! I'm sure if Mom knew you were living here, she would have made you your own box." She tilts her head at me. "Why didn't you tell any of us that you have a roommate? Did you think none of us would find out?"

"Of course, I knew you would find out. Nothing gets past you guys. I was just protecting Paige from your prying for as long as I could."

Tori scoffs. "I'm offended! We don't pry. We lovingly ask questions."

Paige hides a laugh behind the mug at her lips while Tori hops off the stool.

"Well, I wish I could stay and interrogate you some more, Paige, but I have to get going." She lifts up to plant a kiss on my cheek. "I'm sure I'll see you again soon!" She smiles at us both before disappearing out the door.

I shake my head in amusement. "Sorry about that. I wish I could say that will be the last time one of my sisters barges in here, but it happens pretty often. They'll probably stop by more often now that they know there's a gorgeous woman staying here."

The hint of a blush spreads on her cheeks before she picks up her mug and walks toward the boxes on the counter.

"Not a problem. I already like anyone who gives you a hard time. I am going to need to try these cookies, though." She shoots me a smile before taking a bite of a chocolate-chip cookie.

"So, you don't want to share your food with me, but you expect me to share with you? Is that how it's gonna be?"

She finishes the last bite with a smile. "Yup."

"What can I get you?" I ask the two gentlemen across the bar. I scoop ice into two glasses and pour gin and tonic water into both. I slide lime wedges on top, deliver the cocktails, and then scan my eyes down the bar top. There's been a steady stream of customers tonight. There hasn't been an empty stool that's stayed that way for longer than ten seconds.

There's a couple deep in conversation, completely absorbed with each other, absolutely oblivious to the outside world; an older gentleman having an appetizer for one; a group of striking women huddled together, throwing their heads back in laughter; and then there are small and large groups of people squished in between all of them.

"Behind you," Steve calls from my right, passing behind me while carrying three beers. He's another lead bartender like me, so we normally don't work at the same time, but somebody had called in sick, and Steve offered to take the shift. He's damn good at his job and really my only competition for the manager promotion, in my opinion. Unfortunately for me, he's pretty likable, too.

"That blonde over there's been eyeing you for the last hour. You gonna go put her out of her misery?" Steve chuckles, gesturing to the group of women to the left of the bar, the woman in question throwing major vibes my way. She's absolutely stunning, her golden, sun-kissed skin on display with her low-cut black dress.

"Nah…too busy." Truth is, I have no desire to go flirt with her, not when I can't stop thinking about Paige. I was hoping work would be a good distraction from the consuming thoughts about her, but I guess not. It also doesn't help that I've been getting non-stop texts from my mom and sisters asking about her.

I knew when Tori left this morning that it wouldn't be long until they all showed up, but I wasn't expecting it to happen as fast as it did. Tori had only been gone for thirty minutes when Grace all of a sudden 'stopped by.' By four o'clock, when I left for work, Paige had officially met each one of my sisters, my mom, and my niece, Lily. She even met Lily's dog, Archie, that she and Ava were conveniently taking for a walk right by my apartment.

Paige handled it all like a champ, though. She doesn't seem to get frazzled easily, and she fits right in with everybody. She can hold her own with my crazy family, and that definitely doesn't help the whole crush situation. Maybe I really should go flirt with someone else to see if it'll help me get over this thing for Paige. I peer over at the women while I enter my latest drink order, but I just don't have it in me to head over there.

'Before-Paige' Matt would be disappointed in me. But 'After-Paige' Matt just can't seem to shake the hold she has over me.

9

PAIGE

"What do you like on your pizza?" Matt asks, pulling out his phone to place a delivery order. He has the night off from the bar, and Mia's on a date with John, so we're having a low-key roomie pizza-and-Netflix night. It's surprisingly really nice. I've been finding myself actually looking forward to the time I spend with just Matt and me.

He's still cocky and exasperating most of the time, but he's also extremely comfortable to be around, and he makes me laugh —like, really belly laugh, where your abs are sore the next day. Plus, he's unrelenting with the flirting and compliments he throws my way, which you would think would get annoying, but I actually find it endearing. It's easy to be drawn to him. For all of his irritating attributes, his positive ones overshadow them tenfold.

"I'll have Canadian bacon, pineapple, and sauerkraut if they have it. And before you say anything, yes, I know that sounds disgusting. I don't care, and it's delicious. It's my go-to," I reply, trying to hold back a laugh at Matt obnoxiously pretending to gag.

"That is most definitely disgusting. But I'll feed into that gross habit—whatever you want, sweetheart."

My eye catches on the strong line of his jaw as he's focusing down on his phone. His blond hair is ruffled from constantly running his hand through it—a subconscious habit I've noticed that he has. He mindlessly threads his fingers through his hair, coming to rest at the base of his skull, where he then scratches at the back of his neck. I'm surprised that he doesn't have a bald spot where he scratches.

I've seen him do this while watching TV, talking on the phone, or peering into the fridge for food. Not that I'm watching him or anything. I'm still on the friends-only train. It's just damn near impossible to not notice him when he's always around, looking as good as he does.

I scroll through the movie options, trying to find something worth watching, when my gaze shifts to his PlayStation unit and an admittedly impressive display of games that are stacked as high as the TV stand.

"So, what are you, like, twelve years old? What's with your video games?"

He drops his phone, shifts, so he's facing me head-on, and levels me with an intense stare I've yet to see from him. A warmth flushes down my spine as I hold his stare, taken aback by this level of passion. I feel it roll over me like a blanket of heat engulfing me.

"I don't joke about Grand Theft Auto," he says, his voice low and gravelly.

An amused hum leaves my mouth, mentally brushing off the effect his eyes and now voice have on me, my hands flying up in the air.

"Easy…I was genuinely wondering."

Maybe this whole living-together thing isn't such a good idea. Being around him is starting to mess with my head, and it's getting harder and harder to convince myself that he's not a good idea.

"I'm serious, Paige." His eyes are still pinning me in place. "I'm a badass in this game. I take that very seriously. I have a reputation to uphold."

I snort, shaking my head. "God, you guys are all alike, aren't you? My brother plays too. We've played Madden together a few times. It was actually kinda fun," I say with a shrug.

Matt's intense expression shifts into one of shock, his mouth dropping open, his phone falling to the floor.

"Are you kidding me?" He jumps off the couch and starts shuffling through his controllers to untangle the cords. "Not only are you the most stunning woman I have ever laid eyes on, but now you're gonna tell me that you play video games, too? Here," he says, running his finger down the stack of games and pulling out Madden NFL, then he hands me a controller. "We're playing."

"What?"

"I'm not wasting this opportunity. Let's play." The screen lights up with the PlayStation logo before I've even had a chance to reply.

"Do I even have a choice? I wanted to watch a movie."

"Nope." He grabs a throw pillow and barges all the way into my personal space, pushing me forward and shoving it behind my back—and oh my gosh, it's been way too long since I've been this close to a guy because I can't get over how good he smells. A citrus-laced woodsy aroma completely surrounds me. My gaze lifts up to find his eyes darting the other direction. He clears his throat, taking his warm hand off my shoulder.

"Being comfortable is key." He crawls over to his precious chair and shifts side to side a few times, letting his body sink in.

Amused, I sigh and resign myself to the fact that this is what my night has now come to. I don't have the energy to convince him otherwise. He's too stubborn.

"Alright, well, if this is how I'm going to spend my evening, you're buying the pizza."

"Deal," he answers immediately.

I choose the Patriots as my team, and Matt selects the 49ers. We spend the next two hours completely lost in the football world, my team completely dominating his, only taking a break to collect the pizza from the delivery guy. It's been a while since I've played, but it comes right back to me, and I find myself easily getting consumed by it.

"How are you so good at this game?" Matt questions. "I didn't know you were this hardcore!"

"Just one side of me you haven't seen yet, Matty boy."

"Remind me not to piss you off," he says absentmindedly while my player ruthlessly tackles him to the ground. I glance at Matt, whose mouth is hanging slightly open in shock.

I smile smugly while popping the last bite of my pizza into my mouth. Rubbing my hands together to brush off any remaining crumbs, I toss the controller onto Matt's lap as I head to my room for the night.

"It's all yours. Thanks for the pizza!"

'TUTOR NEEDED' the top of the flyer reads, followed by the address for Honu Elementary School. Apparently, they're looking for someone to tutor a few first-graders over the summer. When I saw the flyer this morning at the grocery store, I figured I might as well check it out and offer to help since I still have about seven weeks before I go home. It would be nice to have something to fill my days when Mia's working, and I miss being around kids.

I fold the flyer, shove it in the pocket of my jean shorts, and head up the front steps to the school, admiring the palm trees that surround the brick building. Walking into the office, I'm greeted by a woman peering up from behind the front desk.

"Aloha! How may I help you?"

"My name is Paige Campbell. I'm here to meet with Principal Murphy. We spoke this morning."

"Oh great! Have a seat, please. I'll let her know that you're here."

"Thanks!"

"Hi, Paige! Principal Murphy," a tall blonde woman greets me before I make it to a chair, extending her hand. She has a genuine smile and a kindness to her eyes. I like her already. You can tell a lot about someone by looking in their eyes, and hers immediately put me at ease.

"Pleasure to meet you," I say, returning the handshake. I follow her lead as she walks out of the office, holding the door behind her for me to pass through.

"I'll keep this pretty informal. I saw your teacher credentials that came through, so I'll just show you around the school, show you where you'll be tutoring."

"Perfect! Thanks again. I'm really looking forward to this."

"Absolutely. I'm the one who should be thanking you. You're really helping us out here. All of our teachers are either taking the summer off or already have commitments tutoring other students."

We continue down the long, narrow hallway, then take a right after the cafeteria. On the left is a door that leads to the library, which we walk into. The walls are floor-to-ceiling books, and there are tables scattered around, filling up any leftover space that isn't taken up by book displays. Three large windows line the outer walls, flooding the room with sunlight.

"So, I'll have you do the tutoring in here, if that works for you? Three days a week for a few hours would be wonderful.

Just shoot me your preferred schedule, and I'll work it out with the students. Like I mentioned on the phone, I've got three first-graders who need a little extra help over the summer—two boys and one girl. Two of them are just a bit behind on their reading skills, so that should be pretty straightforward, and then the other boy might need a little bit more creativity when it comes to helping him. He's a sweet boy. He just keeps to himself and doesn't really put much of an effort into his schoolwork. He's a foster child, and he's definitely been through a lot, so we've given him a lot of grace this year. Let me know if you figure out any tricks to get him motivated, because we're kind of at a loss at this point. Not to scare you off... just want to give you a realistic look at what you're signing up for," she says with a sheepish smile.

"No problem. I'm happy to help, honestly." Every single child I've taught has had a different personality and unique challenges. They all learn in different ways. Figuring out a way to connect with a child and cater to their individual learning process is one of my favorite parts of teaching. If I can handle Jackson Peters, I can handle any child.

"Oh, and feel free to take them outside on the school grounds if you'd like. We like to take advantage of the beautiful weather as much as we can. The fresh air is great for the kids!"

"Oh, that's wonderful. I'll definitely do that," I say, happy that I won't need to miss out on any sunshine.

Principal Murphy takes me around the rest of the school, stopping to introduce me to the janitor and a science teacher who's setting up his classroom for a summer program. Otherwise, the building is mostly quiet, as most schools are in the summer.

"So, you're okay starting in a few days?" she asks when we circle back to the front office.

"Absolutely. My schedule's pretty open."

"Great! Nice to meet you, Paige. Thanks again for your help this summer."

With a wave goodbye, I head down the steps outside with a renewed sense of purpose for my time here.

10

PAIGE

"You need to come with me!" Matt yells as he throws the front door open, practically stumbling inside, causing me to nearly spill my bottle of water that I was sipping from.

"What the hell, Matt?" I say, wiping at the drop of water that landed on my shirt. I literally got home fifteen minutes ago. Mia convinced me to go hiking with her today, and it turned into an all-day event. After I showered, I was looking forward to a quiet night in here on the couch.

He slams the door shut and barrels toward me. He grabs my water and screws the cap carefully back on, gently setting it on the table next to the couch where I'm sitting. For someone in a hurry, he sure took his time making sure my water bottle was okay.

"I have to show you something, but we need to go now," he says, impatience building in his eyes.

Okay.

"Can I grab my—"

"Nope," he cuts me off, grabbing my wrist and gently but firmly pulling me off the couch. Laughter bubbles at my throat. I barely have time to slide my sandals on before he swings the door shut behind us.

"This is ridiculous. Where are we going?"

"You'll see."

He still has a firm hold on my wrist as he leads me across the parking lot and down the sidewalk that weaves between the houses of two neighborhoods. The sidewalk eventually morphs into a sandy beach-access trail, which he tugs me down.

"You don't have to pull me, you know. I'll follow. I'm committed now. I'm curious what's so important that you need to basically abduct me from the apartment."

He lets go of my wrist, and my arm swings down, feeling suddenly lighter, still pulsing from his touch.

"Sorry," he mumbles as we curve around a palm tree. My jaw drops open at the stunning sunset that's painted across the sky above the ocean, and my feet stop moving. I'm dazed, momentarily frozen in place. He grabs my wrist again and gently pulls me across the sand, closer to the shore. He sits down on the sand, hand still connected to my wrist. He gives it the slightest squeeze, and I drop down next to him, stretching my legs out in front of me, my arm grazing his.

"Wow," is all I can say. I'm not usually one to be distracted by sunsets, and Mia has certainly dragged me to watch several with her, but oh man, this is something else. I've never seen colors with this intensity before. The turquoise water of the ocean that usually catches my eye when looking at the horizon is muted tonight, almost a pale blue/white as it sits under the most incredible sky. Blue sky morphs into swirls of hot pink, blaze orange, and even a little strip of yellow. Big, puffy, white clouds are spread out seamlessly, and the same bright colors mirror the sky on the ocean surface, creating an absolutely gorgeous sunset.

From the corner of my eye, I can see Matt watching me. I glance over to find his blue eyes studying me.

"This is what you wanted to show me?" I ask, eyes still holding his, starkly aware of the fact that he's watching me and not the sunset he dragged me here to see.

He nods. I glance back at the sky, the corner of my mouth curling into a smile.

"It's beautiful," I say, the words coming out in a soft whisper.

"You're welcome," Matt mutters.

I snort a laugh and shove him playfully with my elbow.

"I saw it when I was driving home and wanted to show you."

I give him a smile. "That's sweet. Mia's gonna be pissed she missed this one." Mia has a thing for sunsets, and I know she would appreciate this even more than I do. They took Quinn car shopping this evening in town, but I hope maybe she'll still see it somehow.

We sit in a comfortable silence for a few minutes, admiring the view, the air so humid it feels like it's pushing against my chest, and sand tickling at the backs of my legs under my light-blue sundress.

"I have a question—purely as a friend, of course." Matt's voice pulls me out of my thoughts, but I keep my eyes fixed on the sky.

"Shoot," I reply.

"Why the hell are you single?" He says it in a slow, genuine way.

I smirk. "I could ask you the same thing."

"I'm serious. I wanna know. Why hasn't some guy scooped you up yet?" Something in his voice makes me turn to him, his gaze firmly on me, his expression void of any sarcasm or humor. Just Matt. The guy underneath the pretty exterior. The guy I'm pretty sure I want more glimpses of.

I let out a sigh, wondering where to start. How much to divulge?

"I guess maybe I'm picky? I go on a lot of dates, so it's not from lack of putting myself out there. I just don't see the point of going on a second date if the first one doesn't blow me away. I guess I'm waiting for that undeniable spark, that connection that leaves you wanting more, you know? I haven't found that yet."

Matt stares at me for a second before slowly nodding his head, like what I said just resonated with him somehow.

"I guess you could say it's hard for me to trust, too." I mindlessly run my hand through the sand. "I've been on a ton of terrible dates, so it's hard for me to get excited about meeting new people. And my dad was in the Air Force, so we moved around quite a bit growing up. Having to start all over at new schools and make new friends every couple years made it hard to even want to try building relationships with people. That's carried over to my adult relationships too. It takes a lot to let people in. Oh, and my college boyfriend cheated on me, so that definitely didn't help."

"Asshole."

I snort. "What about you? You have women literally lined up to date you. You could have your pick. Why haven't you settled down?"

He brings his legs up and rests his elbows on his knees, his triceps flexing involuntarily under his gray T-shirt. He shrugs, looking out at the water.

"A lot of the same, I guess. Haven't found that connection with someone yet. Honestly, there haven't been that many girls that I connect with either—none that actually want to get to know me. Most just want to have some fun. I'm well aware of my reputation. I'm seen a certain way, ya know? I'm just the charming, good-looking bartender who's up for a good time. They don't really see the real me. My relationships have been mostly surface level."

I let the quiet linger for a minute, taking in his honest admission.

"Does that bother you?" I ask.

His brow furrows in thought, shoulders shrugging.

"Yes and no. It bothers me that I'm seen as that superficial, or a womanizer, 'cause I don't see myself that way at all. But I know that the right girl will be able to see through all that. See me for me." He twists his neck to look at me, and I can see the authenticity in his eyes. The walls of arrogance, ego, and charisma are gone. I'm not sure if it's still the humidity or not, but my chest feels like there's a weight lying on top of it, threatening to cut off my breath.

"When was your last relationship?" I ask him, wanting to know more.

"My ex, Alicia, and I split up a couple months ago. We dated for about three months—the most serious relationship I've had in a while. But again, it was pretty surface-level. We both knew it wasn't going anywhere, so we eventually broke it off. I went on a date with this chick, Sabrina, after that. She's friends with a good buddy of mine, Marcus, who I work with, so we see each other occasionally out and about. But it's pretty much fizzled out. She texts me every once in a while when she's drunk and looking to party, but I'm not interested in going down that road." He runs his hand through his hair, scratching at the back of his neck again, and my eyes follow his hand as it moves. I like that he feels comfortable enough with me that he would open up and let me in like this. It's nice to see this side of him.

"I can't blame her for wanting to stay in touch, though. I am a good time." He grins.

Aand he's back.

I shake my head, laughing. "You are something else, Matthew Swanson."

"I know," he says in a way that makes me certain he's heard that countless times before.

"Okay, where do you see yourself in five years?" he asks.

"What is this, a job interview?" I laugh.

"Just getting to know each other." He smiles. "Friends are allowed to ask questions, aren't they?"

"Sure," I laugh. "Let's see...in five years? The only thing I know with certainty is that I'll still be teaching. That's a given. Everything else is up in the air. Maybe married? A kid or two? I'm not really in a hurry for any of that, though. There's so much pressure already on finding the right person—the perfect person. I don't need to put a timeline on it, ya know?"

"I agree. Wise decision," he says.

"What about you?" I ask.

"Hmm..." He looks off at the horizon, where the sun has almost completely disappeared. "I honestly don't know. I would love to get settled in a long-term career, whether that's in the bar world or something totally different. I just know I want to advance from where I am now."

"Really?" That surprises me. He's never mentioned not being happy where he's at. He's always been the epitome of confidence and charisma when I've seen him working. I assumed he loved it.

"Yeah. Other than that, I'd love to travel, get married, have babies—lots of babies." He winks at me.

"Solid plan," I agree with a laugh.

He pushes off the sand to stand, offering his hand to me. I peer up at him, the last remaining sliver of the sunset filling the sky behind him, illuminating his chiseled frame.

I slide my hand into his, feeling the warmth of it wrap around mine to pull me to my feet. As I rise, I can feel his eyes on me, and the moment before letting go of his hand, I lift my gaze to connect with his. He holds my stare, and the intensity in his eyes sends a shiver down my spine, which I'm not quite sure what to do with.

It's become painfully obvious that I'm attracted to him, and he's made it abundantly clear that he's interested in me. He's easy to be around, and getting a glimpse into who he really is beneath the surface intrigues me. Sure, it would be easy to give in to him and have some fun while I'm here, but I'm pretty sure that wouldn't be a smart idea. That kind of temporary fling wouldn't be beneficial for either one of us.

I break eye contact, taking a step back from him. I don't miss the flash of disappointment that crosses his face, but he recovers quickly when he shoots me a gentle smile.

"Thank you for bringing me out here. It was really nice," I say.

"Anything for you, Paige," he says with a sad mix of humor and sincerity.

I resist the urge to loop my arm in his, and we walk back to the apartment side by side.

11

MATT

"I need help, man. I'm in too deep," I tell John. He's sitting next to me on the beach, having just finished a surf session. "She's all I think about. I can't get her out of my head."

John blows out a slow breath, I'm sure contemplating how he wants to play this—how much he wants to get involved. He might be my best friend, but his loyalty is to Mia, Paige's best friend. A tough spot to be in, for sure.

"And you're sure she's not into you?"

"I mean, there are moments when I swear she is, but she keeps insisting we're just friends, so maybe I'm reading it wrong. I don't know how to get over her, dude. I haven't even had her, and she's impossible to shake…ugh," I reply, running my hand down my face.

What started as an innocent crush on Paige has snowballed into an all-consuming-near obsession. It's pitiful, really. I'm not used to going goo-goo-eyed for a chick. If anything, I'm usually the object of someone else's infatuation.

For whatever reason, she just wants to be friends, though, and I need to respect that. I do respect that. I would never actually make a move if she wasn't on board, but dammit, she's hard to get past.

"Maybe she should move out?"

"No." I've never answered a question faster in my life. Living with her and not being able to have her is starting to feel like torture, but the thought of her moving out and not seeing her as much cuts even deeper. Nope, that's definitely not the answer.

"I don't know what to tell you, man. Maybe try and put some distance between you guys? Do something other than hang out at home on your nights off? Go out? You'll still see her plenty, but maybe you need a little time to figure out how to cool off?"

Well, that's a depressing suggestion. I shrug. "Yeah, maybe." I try my best to push my thoughts aside and focus on something else, however futile that will be.

"Enough about me. How are you doing? You still good?" I ask. John was struggling with PTSD last year, and when he finally opened up to me about it, he asked me to be there for him while he got help, to be part of his support system. He didn't necessarily ask me to keep checking on him a year later, but I sure as hell have been and don't plan on stopping.

"I am, man. I really am. I'm in the best place mentally that I've ever been. It's been great having Quinn here, too. Didn't realize how much I missed her."

Some guys might be uncomfortable talking about stuff like this, but only a real man can verbalize his feelings. That's what my sisters tell me, anyway.

"Glad to hear. Let's keep it that way."

"Hey, boys!" Mia calls from our left. I turn to see her and Paige walking along the shoreline with cups of shaved ice in hand. Paige is an absolute vision with her hair in a topknot, oversized shades, taking a bite of her blue-and-red-swirled treat —I've never been more jealous of ice in my life.

"Matt, do you have the night off tonight? We're thinking of going to The Toasted Crab for dinner and drinks. You wanna come?" Mia asks me, squeezing in between John's legs, his arms coming around her like a cocoon.

"I'm in." The words fly out of my mouth before I have time to think.

Shit.

"Yay!" Mia looks pleased, resting her head against John's chest.

Paige takes a seat next to me. "I'm gonna go over to Mia's and get ready with her, so I'll just meet you over there, okay?"

I nod, trying not to make direct eye contact. If she looks into my eyes right now, I'm afraid I would spill my pathetic guts to her. I don't want to make her feel uncomfortable or put her in an awkward situation—not to mention what her rejection would do to me. Maybe John's right. Maybe it would be better if I just try and keep my distance.

"What did you two do today?" John asks, taking a bite of Mia's ice.

"We brought Hazel for a hike this morning. It was really beautiful! And she only complained twice, so I'm calling it a win," Mia chuckles.

Hazel's a sweet kid. She's the daughter of the coffee shop owner in town, Julie. Mia's become close with them since she's been here, and I hear she takes Hazel for the day every once in a while to hang out with her.

"What about you guys?" she asks.

"Just surfing," John says. "We met up a couple hours ago."

I nod in agreement, leaving out the fact that I've spent every single second consumed with thoughts of Paige and why she doesn't want me.

Paige uses my shoulder to push off of as she stands, patting it twice before joining Mia.

"Alright, we're gonna go get beautiful! See you boys in a bit!" she exclaims, joining Mia as they walk in the opposite direction they came from.

I watch them walk away, a sinking feeling in the pit of my stomach. John gives me a sympathetic side glance along with an elbow nudge before getting up. We gather our surfboards and head off the beach. The whole time, I try not to obsess over the warmth of Paige's hand that I still feel on my shoulder.

Well, so much for trying to put space between us. The Toasted Crab is insanely busy tonight, as I knew it would be, given it's a Saturday. I got here a little early to grab my paycheck and check my schedule for next week before John and the girls met me here. My grand plan for the evening was to still participate in conversation, being the gentleman that I am, but also not be completely glued to Paige's side all night. You know, the whole space thing.

That was shot to hell within the first five minutes. They're so busy they had to cram us at a tiny table for dinner, all five of us squished together. Of course, Paige and I wound up next to each other, and all I could think about the entire dinner was her leg that was pressed against mine. John's leg was pressed up against my other leg, but that was more annoying to me than anything.

Not to mention she looks absolutely gorgeous tonight. She has her long brown hair curled, pulled over one shoulder. The reddish tint of her slightly sun-burned skin makes her green eyes pop, and I'm pretty sure she put on red lipstick just to torture me. She's wearing a leopard-print skirt with a white T-Shirt that she tied in a knot, leaving an inch of her bare stomach showing.

She's dancing with Mia and Quinn, occupying every square

inch of the dance floor in the corner of the bar, and I wouldn't be able to tear my eyes away from her even if my life depended on it. There's no live band on the schedule tonight, so the music has been an eclectic mix of songs from every genre you could think of—most of which the girls have chosen themselves on the jukebox.

The song ends, and Paige glances over, catching me staring at her. Goosebumps run down my arms from embarrassment at getting caught, but her hold over me makes it impossible to look away. She mutters something to Mia and then makes her way over to where John and I are leaning against the bar. With each step she takes, closing the distance between us, my heart starts racing faster and faster.

Get a grip, man.

She saunters between John and me, reaching for her drink that we were keeping an eye on. She takes a sip of her Mai Tai and fans herself, out of breath from dancing. Glancing up at me, she shows no trace of surprise at finding my gaze still firmly planted on her.

"Do you ever get sick of this place? We could have picked another bar if you didn't want to come here on your night off," she says, attempting conversation.

I shrug. "I don't mind it, actually. This place is like my second home."

She nods, looking out at the dance floor at Mia and Quinn, who just dragged John out with them. "When do you interview for the promotion?"

"Next week."

"Are you nervous?" she asks, bringing her eyes back to mine. A group of people fill in the space next to her, nudging her closer to me.

"More anxious than anything, ready to know whether or not I got it. As far as I know, it's just Steve and me interviewing, maybe one or two more," I say, trying not to be distracted by how close she is. My heart is pounding so loud, I'm surprised she can't hear it over the music.

"That's a good thing, right? That there's only a few of you? At least there's not a huge group of people to choose from."

"Yeah, I suppose. Except Steve is really fucking nice. And he's a great bartender, so I'm not sure how good my chances are."

She scoffs. "Where's the optimism? Where's the overly confident Matt that we all know and love?"

I chuckle, tearing my eyes away from hers to lazily scan the room. "I guess I just really want it, you know?"

"I'm sure you'll do great. And if it's meant to be, then it'll be. If not, then you move on and find what's actually meant for you," she says cheerfully.

"Oh god, you're one of those, aren't you? One of those glass-half-full kind of girls?" I can't help the grin that tugs at my mouth. Of course, she is. It's fitting and, if it's even possible, makes me like her more.

Before she can answer, Mia grabs her arm and drags her back out to the dance floor while I resume my stance, watching her, with no plans to stop.

12

PAIGE

"Matt's acting weird," I tell Mia and Quinn in the ladies' room. I run my hand under cold water, shake it off and then press at the back of my neck to cool down. "At first, he was all stiff and rigid, hardly saying a word to me, and he kept clearing his throat like he was uncomfortable at dinner. Now, every time I look over at him, he's staring at me. I don't get it." The third Mai Tai I slurped down earlier is making the words spill out of my mouth unfiltered.

"That's probably because he's in love with you," Mia mumbles, washing her hands in the sink next to me.

"Oh, stop," I dismiss her drunken ramblings. "That's just Matt. He'll flirt with anyone in a skirt."

"I hate to break it to you, but Matt hasn't flirted with anyone else the entire night," Quinn pipes in. She runs her hands through her brown hair, teasing the roots to create volume. She bares her teeth in the mirror to check for lipstick stains, then turns to me, leaning her hip on the counter.

"Listen. I've known Matt a long time, and yes, he's a cocky fool most of the time, but I've never seen him look at somebody the way he looks at you. You've got a hold over him, that's for sure." Quinn hasn't had as many drinks as Mia and me, so maybe I should put some weight to her words, but I'm not sure how much of that I can believe. Is it true? Does Matt see me in a different way than the others? Is there something more there? I would be lying if I said I didn't like the way that makes me feel.

"Well, even if that were true, it doesn't matter. I'm only here for the summer," I say. "Yes, he would be THE perfect guy to have a vacation fling with, but I don't want that. Believe it or not, I actually respect the guy, and I don't think I'm capable of doing casual with him. Plus, I don't want to make things awkward—not only for you guys but for the next time I come back to visit, you know?"

Mia slips her arm around my waist, laying her head on my shoulder. "You can't blame him for being obsessed with you. You're easily obsessable."

"That doesn't make any sense," I giggle, squeezing her back, our feet stumbling to stay upright.

"Alright, maybe that's enough Mai Tais, huh?" Quinn ushers us out into the dark hallway. Mia and I fall into step behind her, arms still firmly glued to each other. The muffled sound of music fills the corridor, gradually getting louder with each step, and I can feel the bass thumping in my chest.

After a few steps, I notice a gorgeous woman coming our direction. She has a cute blonde bob that falls just above her shoulders, wearing a black minidress and a scowl on her face that doesn't quite make sense. She must be upset about something.

"Are you Paige?"

Huh?

The mystery woman comes to a stop directly in front of Mia and me, cutting us off and blocking our way out of the hallway. Quinn had raced ahead of us to join some friends at the bar, so she's long gone already.

Is she talking to me?

"Are you Paige?" she repeats, this time her question laced with annoyance.

"Uh, yes. And you are?"

"Doesn't matter." She flips her hair with her hand the exact same way Claire Bingham does in my classroom when she has just the right amount of attitude and wants everyone to know it.

"I just wanted to let you know that I know all about you staying with Matt. For the record, he's off limits. Don't think that just because you live with him that you're gonna get anything from him. He's mine, okay?"

The alcohol swimming in my bloodstream makes her words a little hazy, but as they start to register, so does the threatening look on her face, which makes anger shoot up my spine. Who does she think she is? I've never spoken to her before in my life. She has absolutely no right to tell me what I can or can't do.

"Excuse me?" I half-chuckle, half-demand, partially at the absurdity of it all and partially due to my fuzzy state of mind.

"You heard me—"

"Sabrina!" She's cut off by another woman calling for her.

Sabrina.

Matt's Sabrina.

"Ahh, Sabrina... Matt mentioned you. Funny, he didn't say you were dating, though. In fact, he said you sort of fizzled out." She blanches, and I momentarily regret being so harsh, but that dissipates when she opens her mouth again.

"Clearly, you don't know what you're talking about. I have Matt wrapped around my finger. You'll see," she replies with a smug smile, slowly eyeing me up and down, judging every square inch as she does. Then, she spins and saunters back to join her friend.

"Oh, no she didn't," Mia mutters, then turns to me. "Can you believe her? Are you okay?"

"I'm fine, but wow, that pisses me off. 'You'll see'... really?" Listen, I'm all about the girl code, and I would never go for another woman's man, but none of that applies here. She and Matt aren't even dating. Anger continues to rise, this time up through my chest, getting lodged in my throat.

"You know what? I'm not okay with that." I untangle myself from Mia and start stomping toward the bar, Mia breathing behind my shoulder.

"Where are we going? What are we doing?" she spits out rapidly.

On a mission, I ignore her, making a beeline for Matt, who's leaning an elbow on the bar-top, in conversation with John. He looks exceptionally handsome tonight in tan shorts and a black button-up shirt. I push the thought from my mind—no time for being distracted by his good looks. He glances up to see me barreling toward him. Straightening immediately, concern flashes over his face.

"Dance with me," I demand.

His blue eyes widen, intrigue and confusion flashing briefly until he sets his beer down and dips his head in a curt nod. "Okay," he responds almost immediately. He doesn't skip a beat or question why. He just blindly follows me to the dance floor.

I find an open corner and twist around to face Matt just as the upbeat dance mix that was playing ends, and "Lover" by Taylor Swift starts playing. I wasn't expecting a slow song, and I momentarily falter, mentally cursing whoever chose this song on the jukebox.

Matt's questioning gaze searches mine. Hesitation must be

written all over my face. He gestures to the back door, silently offering to go somewhere else. His body retreats half an inch toward the door, but resolve rushes over me, and I grab his arm.

I can do this. It's just a dance.

I pull his arms around me, wrapping my own around his neck while his hands come to rest firmly on my lower back. My head tilts up slightly to find his eyes burning into mine as we sway slowly side to side, only a couple inches separating us.

"You okay?" he asks, his voice husky.

"Yeah...I met Sabrina," I tell him, hyperaware that his touch is calming the irritation that was all-consuming only moments ago.

"You did?" His brows furrow in confusion.

"Yup. Lovely gal. She staked her claim on you, said you were off limits."

His expression is unreadable for a split second, but the moment realization hits, his mouth slowly lifts up in a cocky grin.

"So you wanted to dance with me to make her jealous?"

Well, when he puts it that way, it seems pretty silly.

"Pretty much," I say with a shrug.

"Well, that's incredibly immature." He pulls me flat against him, my chest pressing against his muscular stomach. "And I'm totally into it. Let's make her real jealous."

The connection takes my breath away, and I have to remind myself to inhale. His hands slide slightly lower to the very tops of my hips. The heat of his touch radiates to every square inch of my body. A fingertip lightly grazes the fabric of my skirt, and it sends a shiver all the way down my arms.

I'm not sure if it's the alcohol or being this close to him that's making me feel like I'm floating, but either way, it's a feeling I slip into, gladly welcoming the blanket of comfort that I feel with his arms around me.

I glance up to lock my eyes with his, and the heat behind

them tells me he might feel the same way. My fingers absentmindedly curl around the back of his neck, my eyes unable to break away from his. In this moment, I forget all about Sabrina—or even anyone else in this bar. It's just me, with my arms around Matt, being serenaded by Taylor Swift.

13

MATT

The song comes to an end, and I mentally beg the jukebox to play another slow song. I don't want to let go of Paige, and I sure as hell don't want her to let go of me. The mental hold she's had over me that I've been trying to shake was only solidified the moment she put her arms around me, transforming quite literally into a physical hold.

My thumb grazes the tiny strip of exposed skin above her skirt, a move that was purely instinctive, and something flashes in her eyes that haven't strayed from mine once. My brain is completely clouded and hyper-focused on one thing—her body firmly pressed to mine—and I don't think my heart has ever raced this fast in my entire life. I could technically blame it on the alcohol that I certainly haven't shied away from tonight, but that would be a lie.

It's Paige.

It's all Paige.

She does something to me that nobody else ever has, and it's starting to really freak me out.

Garth Brooks' "I've Got Friends in Low Places" starts playing, and neither of us makes a move to let go. I take advantage of the slow beginning of the song and keep my hold on her, still swaying. Her eyes move side to side, searching mine for something. She clearly looks like she's as into this as I am. Maybe she's starting to feel something, too. Maybe we could just talk about this like two grown adults.

"Paige…" My voice comes out so low I'm not entirely sure she heard me over the music.

She opens her mouth to say something, but before she can respond, the song picks up, and Mia crashes into Paige, followed by Quinn, separating us with a jolt that every single fiber of my body revolts against. Paige seems to break out of her trance, joining the girls in dancing and singing along, but not before shooting a backward glance at me.

I force myself to move, sulking back to the bar to join John, who looks amused.

"What was that about?" He hides a smirk behind a sip of beer.

I blow out a long breath, trying to slow my heart rate to gain some composure. "I guess Sabrina's here and confronted Paige by the bathrooms. Now, apparently, they're both staking their claim on me." I take a long, slow sip of my beer and shake my head. "I don't know what kind of queen-bee, alpha-female situation that was, but I can't say I minded."

"Yeah, Mia and I saw Sabrina grab her friend and storm out of here when you two started dancing, so I'd say mission accomplished. I gotta say, though, Paige looked pretty into it from where I was standing."

"Right?" I reply. "That's what makes this whole thing so confusing." It would be a lot easier if she would just act outwardly repulsed by me. At least I'd know where she stands.

"I don't envy you, man. I'm so glad I'm past all that 'does she like me' bullshit."

"Yeah, gee, thanks," I grumble as "Pour Some Sugar On Me" comes on the jukebox. "I need another beer."

"Salsa or guac?" Paige doesn't bother to wait for a response before pulling out both containers and tossing them on the kitchen counter. After the Uber dropped us off, we both immediately stumbled to the kitchen in search of an after-bar snack.

"Your mom says, 'Hope you had a great day, sweetie!'" She giggles, peeling the Post-it note off the top of the homemade salsa container.

"Give me that." I grab it from her, crumple it, and throw it in the general direction of the garbage bin, missing completely. Maybe that last drink at the bar wasn't the best idea, but it was necessary to try and drown the effects of dancing with Paige. I can still feel the weight of her arms around my shoulders, her stomach pressed to mine.

I pull the chips out of the cabinet, and we both rest our elbows on the counter, leaning over the gourmet snack we put together. The entire counter is wide open with space, yet we're about as close as you can get, our forearms brushing against each other as we dunk the chips. Now that we've experienced what it feels like to be close, it's like our bodies just naturally gravitate toward each other, an invisible force pulling us together.

"This is good." She pops a salsa-laden chip into her mouth while I hum in agreement.

"I think I prefer salsa over guac," I say. "You just can't beat it. You got the tomatoes, the onion, that green stuff in there. The chip doesn't break when you scoop it out. So good."

"Yeah, but guac is in a league of its own. It's so creamy and smooth. The flavor. Mmm. Yummy," she muses at the chip in her hand before shoving it in her mouth. "Too bad we don't have any queso."

My phone dings with a notification in my pocket. I brush excess salt off my fingers and grab my phone. The screen displays a message that tells me my mom just played her turn in Scrabble. I try to clear it away but not before I hear Paige gasp.

"Oh my god, are you playing Scrabble?"

"No," I huff, trying to shove the phone back in my pocket. She laughs and grabs at my arm, trying to pry my phone free.

"Let me see!"

I chuckle, letting her body lean against mine, her hand still clutching at my arm. I move my phone up and down, dodging her arm as she grabs for it. I'm loving every single second of her hanging on me until, eventually, I give up and let her take it.

"You play on the Scrabble app against your mom?" She suddenly stops moving, drops her hands to her sides, and looks up at me with the cutest puppy-dog eyes I've ever seen. "Why is that the most adorable thing I've ever heard?"

I'll tell ya something else that's adorable—the way she's looking at me right now. Her eyes narrow, and the expression on her face morphs into a playful one.

"I bet she's kicking your ass. Do you even know how to spell words?" she teases with a giggle.

"I know plenty, thank you very much." Not my best comeback, but she's throwing everything off kilter here. I'm in brand-new territory with her.

"Yeah, I'm sure you do," she laughs. "I bet your highest-scoring move is *beer*. Or *mommy*." She erupts into a fit of laughter, collapsing over the counter as she's clearly not able to laugh and stay upright at the same time.

"Is that funny?" I can't help but laugh at her when she's completely unhinged. Drunk Paige is definitely taking the number-two spot on my list of favorites, right behind Morning Paige.

"Uh-huh," she confirms, trying to catch her breath. "It's hilarious, actually." She brings a finger to swipe under her eye.

"You know I'm just teasing." She sets her hand on the outside of my forearm.

I grin back at her. "You can tease me all day long if you want —actually, you already kind of do," I muse.

"I know. Sorry," she says, although not at all convincingly. Then, she lets out a big sigh, turning toward the chips. "Well, I'm gonna call it a night."

I help her put the food away and then gesture down the hall with my arm, letting her go first. I can't help but stay just a half-step behind her, close enough to smell the hint of strawberry in her hair.

"Are you walking me to my room?" She throws a skeptical glance behind her shoulder.

"I don't know why I need to keep reminding everyone that I'm a gentleman," I reply flatly.

Approaching her doorway, she suddenly stops and spins around. I barrel to a stop just before running into her completely. She's close enough now that all I'd need to do is reach my hand out three, maybe four, inches, and I'd be grazing her hip.

"Matt?" she asks quietly, looking up at me.

"Hmm," is all I can mutter with her this close.

"I'm sorry for dragging you out to dance tonight. I usually don't get caught up in girly drama like that, but I couldn't seem to help it this time." The corner of her mouth twists with guilt, and her shoulders lift in a shrug.

The hum of electricity between us pulls me an inch closer. "You don't need to apologize for that."

"I don't?" She scans my face—searching for what, I don't know. I search right back, following the line of a strand of hair that fell over her cheek, close to her lips, and I wonder what it would be like to kiss her.

"No. I liked dancing with you," I force out.

She pulls the strand of hair behind her ear with her finger at the same time I say, "Paige—"

Once again, I'm interrupted. This time, by Paige pressing her lips to mine. It takes my body a mere second to register what's happening, but I quickly recover, bringing my hands immediately to her hips. She wraps her hands around each bicep, gently squeezing as our lips push against each other.

She slides her hands up my arms and around my neck, sending goosebumps across my skin. I bring my hands up the sides of her body, slip them around to her back, and then back down to rest on the curve of her butt. I gently turn her to the left and walk her backward until she's pressed flat against the wall, my weight pressed firmly against her.

She squeezes her arms tighter around me, pressing her chest to mine as the heat between us becomes almost overwhelming. We spend the next few blissful minutes making out against the wall until, eventually, I break away, giving us both a chance to catch our breath.

I search her eyes for any hint of what she's thinking, but she just stares at me, her chest rising and falling. We stay that way for what seems like forever, my arms still firmly wrapped around her.

Then, she slides her arms down my sides, pausing by my ribs, and gives me a small smile. She gently pushes me away and gives me a quick squeeze.

"Goodnight, Matt," she whispers, untangling herself from me and disappearing into her room. I can only stare after her, my body feeling the loss of hers. She gently closes the door before I can mutter a single word.

14

PAIGE

The butterflies in my stomach get more intense as I slowly come out of the haze of my dream. I'm completely overwhelmed at the memory of our kiss last night. My nerves are buzzing, heart is pounding, just from remembering his lips on mine, his hands on my waist. It's been a long time since I've felt chemistry like that with someone, and admittedly, it felt good. Really good.

Except, another part of me feels like it was a line that we probably shouldn't have crossed. We're friends, not to mention roommates, who will be seeing each other all the time while I'm here. If things got messy with us, it would affect our whole friend group.

Also, I'm only here for a little while. I'll be going home eventually, so what's the point of starting something with him? It would only make things awkward the next time I come back to visit.

I groan into the pillow, dreading having a conversation with Matt.

Coffee first.

I roll onto my side, pushing against the mattress to hoist myself off with another groan, this one coming out involuntarily. The pounding behind my eyes is another clear reminder that I definitely should have stopped after two cocktails last night.

After exhaling a calming breath, I open the door and head for the kitchen. My heart skips a beat when I see Matt sitting on a stool, sipping coffee. He's wearing sweatpants without a shirt, and I can see every well-defined muscle on his back.

Not helping.

When he turns at the sound of my shuffling feet, he pushes his lips together, attempting to hide a laugh.

I get it. I'm admittedly a disheveled mess in the mornings, and when I'm hungover, I'm on a whole other level. I attempt to flatten my hair with my fingers but quickly give up. What's the point?

"Morning." My voice comes out groggy. Matt points to the coffee sitting on the counter that he made for me. It's a small act, one he's made several mornings, but this time, it feels different. The whole apartment feels different, like everything has woken up somehow, a new energy buzzing through the walls. The electricity in the air mirrors the vibration coming from Matt's eyes as he scans mine, so many questions hidden behind them.

"Morning," he responds. "There's coffee and an Advil next to it if you need it."

"Thanks," I breathe, swallowing the medicine with a gulp of coffee. I lean across the counter directly in front of where Matt's propped up on the opposite side, facing me.

I take another sip of coffee and will the caffeine to make me feel a little more alive and ready for this conversation.

"So…should we talk about the elephant in the room?" I peer at him from behind my mug.

His eyes hold mine, and he pushes his lips together and nods, bracing himself for whatever direction this is going to go.

"Sure."

"Listen," I start. "I like you, Matt. I really do. I have a lot of fun with you."

"But?" I watch as his eyes cloud over slightly.

"I don't want to ruin our friendship. I'm only here for a little while. I don't want to make things messy by crossing that line. You know what I mean?"

He lets out a deep sigh, slowly nodding his head. "I do. Obviously, I would love to explore something more with you, but I hear what you're saying. And I respect that." I can see the disappointment written all over his face, but he smiles, attempting to put me at ease, which I appreciate.

A grateful smile crosses my lips. "Thanks for being so mature about this."

"Mature is my middle name," he says, and I snort out a laugh. "Besides, if I remember correctly, you were the one who kissed me, so…"

"Oh, is that right?"

"Mmhmm," he hums. "I apologize for being so tempting. I'll do my best to tame it down, for your sake."

"That would be great," I say with an eye roll. I'm grateful that he isn't making this a big deal, and we can go right back to how things were.

He taps the counter with one hand, grabbing his mug with the other.

"I'm off to surf with John for a while today, and then I work a shift at the bar tonight. I shouldn't be back late."

I nod. "I start tutoring today, so I probably won't see you until later, then."

His eyes linger on me for a beat, then he retreats to his room.

I finish my coffee and then take a shower to start getting ready for the day. When I'm all ready to head out the door, I notice that Matt's already gone. Just to make sure we really are alright, I pull the Post-its out of the drawer where his mom keeps them and leave him a note that says, *Let me know when you need help figuring out the next Scrabble word. Paige.*

"This is Ms. Campbell. She's going to be your tutor for the next several weeks, okay?" Principal Murphy says to the three kids who—judging by their faces—this is the last place they want to be. Three heads nod slightly, as well as a frown and an eye roll. I get it. If I were a kid living in Hawaii, I would spend my entire summer in the ocean or a pool. School would be the last place I would want to be, too.

"Paige, this is Ruby, Elliot, and Graham. I'll leave you to it. Let me know if you need anything. I'll be in the office." Principal Murphy leaves with a smile. I turn to my three new friends and have a seat at the round table next to them. I always like to get on my students' level and be as approachable as I can be.

"Hi, guys. I'm Paige. I think we're gonna have a good time this summer together. I love to have fun, so I'll try and make learning as fun as I possibly can, okay?"

Ruby eyes me head to toe and then seems to come to some sort of conclusion, annoyance disappearing from her face, replaced with a smile. She nods at me, tucking a loose strand of black hair behind her ear that fell out of her topknot.

"I like to have fun, too," she says, her smile widening to show me the gap from her missing front tooth.

"Well, we're gonna get along great, then."

Graham shoots his hand up in the air.

"Graham, you don't have to raise your hand if you have a question. Go ahead and just ask. Let's just keep indoor voices while we're inside. Do you have a question?"

"Yeah, how much longer are we going to be here?" His delivery doesn't come off as rude, just genuine curiosity oozing out of his blue eyes. I stifle a laugh.

"We have about an hour and fifty minutes left, buddy. Should we get to work?"

I open the folder Principal Murphy had given me with stats and info on each of the students as well as areas to focus on this summer. I can tell by the end-of-the-year grades that Elliot is the one who's in foster care and not showing an interest in school. He stares at the table with a far-off look in his eyes, his thin frame taking up only a fraction of the chair he's sitting on.

There's a stack of reading comprehension worksheets in the back, so I pull three of those out and set one in front of each of them. Ruby and Graham open their pencil pouches to pull out a pencil and start writing their names at the top of the page. Elliot sulks down a little farther in his seat, pushes his glasses higher on his nose, then crosses his arms.

"Elliot, do you need a pencil? I have plenty of extras."

He meets my eyes for a quick second and then looks back down with a shrug of his shoulders. He looks uncomfortable, and I get the feeling that questioning him might make him feel like the spotlight is on him, so I just slide my pencil to him without another word, then read off the directions at the top of the page.

Ruby and Graham busy themselves with the questions while Elliot doesn't move a muscle. I decide not to push him too hard, especially on the first day. Maybe he needs to get used to me a little bit, see if I'm someone he can trust. Get to know me a little more.

Once we've gone through that worksheet, I collect the two sheets from Ruby and Graham, as well as the blank one from Elliot, not giving it any specific attention. I grab a book from my stack of books that I pulled from the shelves before the students arrived.

"Ooh, are you gonna read that one to us, Miss C?" Graham asks excitedly, seeing that it's a book about dragons.

"I thought I would! It looks like a good one, doesn't it? I'll read one today, and then maybe next time, you can read a book to us. How does that sound?" He and Ruby both enthusiastically nod their heads and then lean forward in their seats across the table to get a closer look at the pictures.

Elliot remains staring at the table with a blank look, and something in my heart breaks a little bit for him. I don't know anything about his story or what he's been through, but something tells me he's used to being ignored—just going through the motions of being wherever he's told to be but far from being present or engaged in the moment. That would be my guess, anyway.

I open the book and make sure it's visible to all three of them, even though only two are looking. When I get to the end of the book, I close it and gently lay it on top of the table.

"Wow! That was so cool! The part where Jett jumps on the dragon's back, and they get into a sword fight with that other guy... Woosh! Woosh!" Ruby wields her fake sword at Graham, who blocks with his own imaginary sword, and the sounds coming from them make me laugh.

"Alright, settle down. Let's do a couple more worksheets before time's up for today." I pass out the next worksheet, wait a few moments until Ruby and Graham are finished, then I collect all three. The last sheet that I pass out has math problems listed on the front side, with a graphing chart on the back. I go through the directions, and I'm surprised to see Elliot pick up his pencil out of the corner of my eye. I try not to let him catch me watching him, so I busy myself with returning the books that I had picked out.

My mind is tempted to drift to Matt, and the feel of his hand on my hip threatens to distract me more than once, but I push it out of my head. This is not the time or the place to be thinking about that.

When I sit back down, I see that Ruby and Graham are almost finished. Elliot has the very first math problem done, and now he's scribbling a very impressive drawing of a dragon in the side margins. A surge of pride rushes through me, pleased with the fact that he actually completed one problem—correctly, too.

"Do you like dragons?" I ask him gently. He stops drawing, looks up at me, and then back down just as quickly. He shrugs his shoulders, resuming his drawing.

"Alright, guys. Time's up for today. Principal Murphy said to head back to the office. That's where you'll be picked up. Thanks for hanging out with me. I can't wait to see all of you in just a couple days! If it's not too hot, maybe we'll do our work outside," I tell them, grabbing my folder, patiently waiting for them to gather their belongings.

Ruby and Graham skip down the hallway. I stay behind a few feet, just far enough to still keep up with them but also stay connected to Elliot, who's lagging behind. At the office, Ruby and Graham wave and head out with their parents.

"You ready to head inside for a bit?" Principal Murphy asks Elliot. "There are some crackers waiting for you in my office."

Elliot doesn't show anything in response. He just heads toward her office without a sound. I wait for him to be out of earshot.

"Does he not have someone coming to pick him up?"

"He does. His foster parent will be here eventually, but she almost never shows up on time. She left a message with my receptionist, something about running some errands. Who knows? I'm happy to let him stay for a while when needed. It's become our norm after school. He's gotten used to my office."

My chest feels tight as I nod and hand her my tutoring folder for her to keep for next time.

"Oh, wait!" I take the folder back and grab Elliot's worksheet that has his drawing on it. This one's coming with me. I have a feeling he doesn't have anybody in his life who cares enough to hang onto his schoolwork. I wave goodbye and head out of the building to head home and place this worksheet directly on the fridge.

15

MATT

"Well, Matt, everything looks good. Obviously, you've been a valuable part of my team for a while now." Mike taps the stack of papers in front of him on his desk, signaling the end of my interview. "For what it's worth, I think you'd make a great manager."

"Give it to me straight, man. What are my chances?" The back corner of the chair digs into my shoulder as I shift in my seat. I wouldn't necessarily say I was nervous for this interview, but I can't help but feel a few jitters when the course of my professional life could potentially be altered.

He sucks in a breath of air through the side of his upturned mouth. "I won't lie to you and give you false hope. I've had a few people interview already. You're my last one."

Shit.

I thought it was just Steve and me that applied. I wonder who else interviewed.

"But I'd say you're definitely a top contender." He looks me straight in the eyes. "You have a skill, that's for sure. You should feel good about how far you've come as a bartender these last few years."

"Thanks. I've been doing my best." I try to keep the smugness from being noticeable in my voice. It goes without saying that I'm a fairly confident guy, but of course, it's always nice to hear compliments from someone else—especially when it's about work and coming from a guy I respect so much.

"I'll keep you posted on my decision. It should be within the next couple weeks." He extends his hand, which I firmly shake.

"Sounds good. Thanks for the opportunity, man."

I'm staying to work a shift, so I head out of the office and straight for the bar. I feel pretty good about how the interview went, but I still blow out a deep breath to let go of any lingering tension I might be holding onto.

"How'd it go?" Marcus asks as I slip my phone into my pocket and key my code into the computer to clock in. Marcus is one of my good buddies. I always look forward to shifts when we get to work together.

"I think it went alright. I didn't fumble over my words or say anything inappropriate, so that's a miracle in itself."

Marcus grunts in agreement while I start preparing some juices and mixers for the afternoon. I scan the room to get a feel for how busy it is. The lunch rush has cleared out, and there are a few open tables, which usually hints at a slower time of day.

Now that the interview isn't occupying my mind anymore, my thoughts shift to the singular thing that has completely consumed my brain the last two days.

Paige.

Kissing Paige.

Touching Paige.

If I thought I had it bad before, that kiss sent me flying right over the edge. There is no hope of 'getting over' her—not while she's on the same island. All I can do is suck it up and deal with it while she's here. As impossible as that seems, I respect her wishes. Although, I don't understand why her wishes don't include me—and another make-out session.

I mindlessly wipe the bartop down while I think back on every interaction I've had with her since the kiss. After we had our talk yesterday morning, I went surfing with John and tried to sweat out the sting of rejection. It didn't help much, but I did let the waves crash over me repeatedly—also didn't really help, but at least it distracted me a bit.

When I got back from work last night, she had just come out of the bathroom with only a towel wrapped around her. I'm surprised my eyes didn't completely pop out of their sockets. That was complete torture, to say the least. She hurried down the hall to her room with a quick wave goodnight. I huffed into the kitchen and tried to distract myself by stuffing my face with pasta.

I saw her again this morning for about a half hour in the kitchen before she ran off to meet up with Mia. Something about going for a bike ride. Nothing was weird or awkward, which is good. If anything, things are only off because I can see in the way she looks at me that she feels this, too. Maybe not to the extent that I do, but it's there. There was a moment where our eyes connected over our muffins, and I can almost guarantee she was thinking about my hands on her. I know I was.

"So, I saw Sabrina yesterday," Marcus says, pulling me out of my thoughts. He and Sabrina are pretty close. He's the one who initially introduced us. He smirks, running the drying towel in his hand around a martini glass. "Boy, did you make her mad. She was all in a huff about you and Paige."

I shrug, tossing the rag in the sink. "Didn't mean to make her upset, but Sabrina and I aren't together. Whatever we had is over. She can't just go around threatening any girl I'm interested in."

"Hey, I get it. I'm not saying she's right, but you know how she gets. She always attaches hard to the guy she's into. I'm sure it'll be someone new next week, now that she knows you're taken." He shakes his head in amusement.

I don't feel the need to correct Marcus and let him know that Paige and I aren't dating. It's a fact that I'm still trying to wrap my head around, and talking about it won't change a damn thing.

There's a sudden rush of customers at the bar, so fortunately, the conversation is shelved for now. I turn to the couple that just sat down, attempting to push Paige to the back of my mind.

"What the hell happened in here?" I pause immediately after pushing open the apartment door. Clothes are scattered all over the kitchen table, makeup covers the living room floor, and my kitchen counter is now a decent substitute for a hair salon. A hairdryer and several curling irons are taking up all the outlets while brushes and hair pins cover any remaining open space.

"Oh, hey!" Paige calls from the kitchen. She's standing next to Mia, pouring blended margaritas into six glasses.

"You want one?" she asks, holding up a glass. "Your sisters are here. They're in my room."

"All of them?" I wave off the margarita.

"Yeah! So, Tori has a date tonight with some guy her friend is setting her up with. She had nothing to wear, so Grace offered to let her borrow something of hers, and then Emily was offended that she wasn't asked to do her makeup, and it all snowballed from there. They're helping Tori try on outfits in my room. I'm sure they'll be right out."

"Oh god, they added you to their group text? Since when?"

"Oh, I've been part of that chain for a while now. We've all bonded over our mutual love of making fun of you," she says with a smile so sweet I can't help but laugh. I let out a resigned sigh and press my palms into my eyes, mentally preparing for the feminine tornado I just walked into.

"Hi, Matthew!" Grace says, the first to come out of Paige's room. She extends her arms out Vanna White style, and Tori comes strutting down the hallway, followed by Ava and Emily.

"Ooooh! I LOVE that dress!" Mia squeals.

Tori does a twirl when she makes it to the living room, and Ava comes behind her to fix the strap in the back.

"Eh, it's not my favorite," Emily chips in, her eyes studying the dress, her finger tapping at her chin.

"Yeah, same. I think I like that blue one better," Tori muses, taking a sip of her margarita.

"Oh! I have the perfect romper! Come on!" Grace leads the way back down the hall, Tori following close behind. I grab a beer out of the fridge and have a seat on the stool in the corner to take it all in.

"You're staying?" Mia asks in surprise. "I figured you'd hole up in your room to get away from all this girly stuff."

"What, you think this bothers me?" I take a sip. "This is literally my entire life. I don't remember a single time when I wasn't smothered by women—except maybe college, but I had a posse of women around for different reasons then." I shoot Mia a wink.

"Gross." Mia frowns, and Paige rolls her eyes.

Tori emerges, wearing a black romper, which they all ooh and ahh over, then Emily starts handing her accessories to try on while Grace runs her fingers through her blonde curls.

"So, who's the guy, T?" I ask, figuring now's as good a time as any to get some dirt on him.

"You don't know him," Tori says, brushing me off.

"Hey, it's my duty as your brother to sufficiently interrogate him. In fact, I should really meet him in person, see if he scares easily. Where are you going to eat?"

She snorts. "Like I'd tell you. He's a nice guy. You don't have to worry."

"Well, unfortunately, you don't have the best track record. Your judge of character seems to be a little off…remember Elijah?"

"I choose not to think about him. Thanks for bringing him up." She glances at Mia and Paige.

"I haven't had the best of luck with guys."

"Oh, Paige can relate! She's been on every bad date in the book!" Mia chimes in. "Which just proves how small men's brains are. I mean, what guy in his right mind wouldn't be falling at her feet? Just look at her!"

Paige glances at me from behind her margarita glass, and I hold her stare for as long as she'll let me. She gives me a half-smile. What I wouldn't give to know what she's thinking.

Mia's right, though. I'd fall at her feet, too, if I thought it would help at all. But my mom raised me right, and if a girl says no, then that's the end of it. The ball is in her court now. All I can do is pray like hell that she'll change her mind.

"Okay, this is the one! I gotta hurry. I don't want to be late," Tori says.

"Is he picking you up, or are you meeting there? Do you have your mace spray?" I ask, which earns me multiple eye rolls and no decency of an answer.

"Alright, you go ahead," Ava says. "We'll clean up!"

"Have fun! Let us know how it goes!" Emily calls after Tori as she rushes out the door.

"Phew," Grace lets out a sigh and then turns to me. "See, Matt. That's the amount of work that women put into getting ready for a date. You better appreciate that."

Now it's my turn for an eye roll, and I head over to the fridge to see what food they brought over this time. It's just a given that they did, after all.

"There's sushi from the market in there for you, and Mom

baked you some fresh bread—on the counter there," Emily says, unplugging the hair dryer and curling iron and then turning to Mia and Paige. "We're gonna go out to dinner. Do you guys wanna join us? Girls' night?"

"Ooh, yes!" Mia and Paige squeal simultaneously. Paige seems to take pity on me. "Do you want to join our girls' night?"

"Oh, don't be so polite," Ava retorts. "The last thing he'd want to do is join us."

"She's right. I'll pass. Have fun, though." I pop a sushi bite in my mouth and watch patiently as they gather their things, fix each other's hair, and head out.

"Bye, Matt! Make good choices!" Emily calls, shutting the door behind her.

I breathe out a sigh, relishing in the quiet state of my apartment, wondering if I should attempt to go out, too. I could call John or Brian or maybe head to the beach.

None of that sounds appealing, though, so I bring my sushi and beer to the couch, flipping through the movies, wondering what Paige would choose to watch if she were here.

16

PAIGE

"Summer really is the best time to snorkel Shark's Cove. In the winter months, the swells are too big, making it dangerous to snorkel in this particular spot," the guide, Ryan, tells us as we stand on the beach overlooking the rocky entrance to the popular snorkel spot.

"I highly recommend wearing water shoes as those rocks can get pretty slippery on your way in. But once you get past the entrance, it's smooth sailing from there. Shark's Cove is one of the top twelve snorkeling spots in the world. Your readers won't be disappointed."

Mia's writing an article on Ryan's business that does sightseeing tours around a few key spots on the North Shore of the island—Shark's Cove being one of the stops. This was definitely one of Mia's projects that I wanted to tag along for. I'm all for exploring and learning as much as I can about Oahu while I'm here.

"Come down this way, and I'll introduce you to some of the food-truck owners on the beach."

I pull my hair up in a bun as we follow Ryan, the heat from the sun making my hair feel heavy and sticky. When he's just out of earshot, Mia whispers in my ear,

"Okay, but do you want to kiss him again?"

I quiet her with a shush and bat her hand away from my arm. I waited to tell Mia about the kiss with Matt—I'm not sure why —but I finally caved and told her on the hour-long drive over here. Most definitely a mistake, as that's all she seems to want to talk about now.

I knew I would get grilled about it, and honestly, that's probably why I kept it to myself at first. I can't even really make sense of this Matt thing myself, so I don't have any decent answers to her questions. Was the kiss amazing? Yes. Do I want to do it again? More than I'd like to admit. But am I convinced that it would be a good idea? No.

Mia already knows all of that, and she knows the overall gist of my situation, but that hasn't stopped her from trying to get more details.

"Did he grab your butt?" she whispers. This time, I'm pretty sure Ryan heard her, judging by the smile he's trying to hold back. I jog a few steps to catch up with him.

"So, the Pali Lookout is the last stop on your tour, right?" I ask him, effectively ignoring Mia. We walk and chat, then eventually stop at the food trucks, where Mia pulls herself together enough to ask him the last couple of questions on her list.

After we say goodbye to Ryan, Mia and I grab some shrimp tacos and sit on the beach.

"You're really not gonna give me any of the dirty details?" she asks, taking a bite.

"Nope. Listen, I'm doing my best to try and not think about Matt. I really do like him, and obviously, I'm attracted to him.

The more I think about him, the harder it's getting to convince myself not to go there."

"So, why not go there?"

"Mia…I respect your life choices, and obviously, I'm happy for you and John, but I'm not going to move to Hawaii for a guy, especially one I would have only dated for a month or two. That's just not realistic for me. So what's the point, you know?"

"What if he turns out to be the love of your life?" she asks.

"I highly doubt it. Plus, I feel like I wouldn't know if he was the love of my life in that short of a time, ya know? It takes me a while to really let people in, and we don't have that kind of time here."

"I mean, I get it. And I support whatever you want to do, you know that." She pops the last bite of her taco in her mouth.

I crumple the taco wrapper in my hands and push myself up to stand.

"Come on, I need to shower when we get back before I tutor this afternoon."

She wipes the sand off her shorts and falls into step next to me as we walk off the beach.

"Okay, did everybody pick a book?" I ask Graham, Elliot, and Ruby at the door of the school library. Three heads nod, and we make our way through the halls to the back door that leads outside. I push the door open and immediately feel the heat hit me and the sun glare in my eyes. I scan the grounds to see what we have to work with.

There's a large playground on the left, surrounded by a few benches. To the right of the swing set is a basketball court with a few picnic tables sitting a few yards from that. I spot a large palm tree that's casting a decent amount of shade, so I head in that direction.

"Everybody have a seat on the ground here. I'll have each of you read the book you brought to the rest of us. Maybe if we get done in time, you can play for a few minutes on the playground, okay? Who would like to go first?"

Ruby shoots her hand straight up in the air as fast as lightning, which clearly wasn't necessary since neither Graham nor Elliot raised theirs.

"Ruby, go ahead." She flips the book open and proceeds to read her story about the princess that enters a cake-baking competition. She gets stuck on a few words, and it takes her a little while to get through it, but eventually, she flips the book closed.

"Great job, Ruby!" I give her a high-five, relishing the look of pride on her face.

Graham volunteers to go next, and he reads us his story about a kid who goes to baseball camp. After he closes the book and finishes telling us about his own baseball team that he's on, we all turn to Elliot.

"Elliot, are you ready to read?" I ask him. He gives a slight shake of his head, keeping his focus down on the grass in front of him, his light-brown hair dropping over his eyes.

"Elliot never reads in class," Ruby says. "He hardly talks at all."

"That's alright," I reply, noticing the hint of red on Elliot's cheeks. My chances of getting through to him might be better if we don't have an audience.

"Ruby and Graham, since you finished your reading, you two can go ahead and play for a while. I'll let you know when it's time to head back inside."

I barely finish the last word, and they're already off, racing to the slide. I move so I'm sitting cross-legged directly across from Elliot.

"What's the book about?" I ask him, dipping my head lower so I can make eye contact. The way he eyes me suspiciously makes me wonder how often anyone makes a point to get down on his level—or how many even look in his eyes. Still, he doesn't respond, only shrugs.

"Can I see it?" I ask, holding out my hand. He hands it to me, and I open it to flip through the pages. I move to sit next to him, still giving him space but close enough that he can see the book.

"Oh, cool. Another book about dragons. I like this red one. He looks pretty fierce," I say, keeping my attention on the book. "Do you have a favorite one?"

Out of the corner of my eye, I can see him scan my face, maybe determining what my motives are. I continue slowly flipping the pages, commenting on the pictures.

"This one has green eyes, just like me. Ooh, this one has red eyes. That's pretty creepy."

I can see the smallest hint of a smile on his lips.

"Look how big the wings are on this one. I bet he can fly pretty fast!" I say, pointing to the picture, then continue flipping the pages. I'm trying to just be here with him without asking any questions or putting him on the spot. Show him that he can trust me, that I'm here to help him learn.

I get to the last page, which shows three dragons standing on top of a cliff. I try not to react at all when I see Elliot point to the book.

"I like the blue one. He's the smartest dragon," he says quietly. I nod my head in approval.

"He looks pretty cool."

My heart swells at this moment of connection. He pushes his glasses higher on the bridge of his nose.

"Can you read any of these words?" I ask him casually.

He nods. "I can read all of them."

Surprised, I point to a word. "What's this word?"

"Fire," he whispers.

"This one?" I point to another.

"Entangle."

"Good job! That's a really hard word!" I'm seriously impressed at his reading abilities. Clearly, he has the skills. He just doesn't like to participate in group settings like school.

I really want to see if I can get further with him, but the timer on my Apple Watch goes off, indicating our tutoring time's up for the day.

"Thanks for looking at this book with me," I tell Elliot. "I can't wait to see what book you pick out next time. I bet it'll be a super-cool one." The corner of his mouth lifts up in a hesitant smile. "Should we head inside?"

We gather our books, call for Ruby and Graham, and head back inside. At the front office, Ruby and Graham race off with their parents, and Principal Murphy greets Elliot and me. Elliot walks right past her and into her office without a word.

"How's he doing?" Principal Murphy asks me.

"He's pretty reserved and quiet, but if I get him alone, I can see parts of him starting to open up. I think he knows quite a bit more than he lets on school-wise. He's just reluctant to participate," I tell her.

She pushes her lips together and nods. "That's kind of what I've gathered, too. I've been trying to get his foster mom in here for a meeting so we can get on the same page about his education, but she hasn't seemed interested."

"Do you mind me asking how he ended up in foster care?"

She blows out a steadying breath, making sure he's not within earshot. "Well, I can't disclose details, only what's public knowledge. His parents didn't really give him a great start in life to begin with. Supposedly, they dabbled in drugs, couldn't hold down a steady job. They moved from place to place when they couldn't afford rent. His mom passed away when he was four or five—cancer, I believe. Her death sent his dad spiraling further into drugs, and he got involved in drug trafficking. He was arrested a few years ago. He's in there for life."

"Wow." It's hard to ignore the pit in my stomach. "That's so sad. He's such a sweet kid."

She hums in agreement. "He is. I try my best to give him a decent school life, but there's not much more that I can do. Anyway, I better get in there. Thanks for your help today." She waves me off and disappears into her office.

I open the door and sit on the top step outside the building to call an Uber. While I wait, I think about Elliot and his story. I'm determined to do the absolute best I can to get him interested in school and willing to participate in second grade this fall. It's the least I can do. Life's already dealt him some low blows and assigned him unfair labels. He doesn't need 'school dropout' to be added to the mix.

17

MATT

"Hey," Paige says, eyes glued to the TV as I close the front door behind me. "How was work? Find any new groupies today?"

A warmth runs through my chest, and I can't help but smile. I love having someone here to ask me about my day, and more specifically, I love that it's Paige I'm coming home to. Maybe I'm a glutton for punishment, but I can't help it.

Whether we're teasing each other, making the other a cup of coffee, or mindlessly chatting about our days, I've gotten used to having her here. She might not want to date me, but at least we enjoy each other's company.

It's gonna be really hard when she leaves, but I try not to think about that. My brain doesn't want to acknowledge the fact that she won't be here when summer's over—not yet, anyway.

"It was great. No new groupies. It was a slow afternoon," I say bluntly, noting her sarcastic nod. She's wearing tight black biker shorts with an oversized light-blue T-shirt on top, and I know she's probably trying to be comfy, but she's also so incredibly sexy it hurts.

I toss my keys on the kitchen table, grab a beer from the fridge, and then find a spot to sit right next to her on the couch, bypassing my chair altogether.

"How was your day?" I ask, a level of comfort settling between us that I've come to crave.

"It was good!" She doesn't take her eyes off *Wheel of Fortune* but continues talking. "Mia and I went to the beach to relax and stopped at Marty's to say hi. It was freaking hot, though. We both had enough sun for the day, so we went our separate ways to relax in the air conditioning." She gestures at the TV. "You're looking at my evening right here."

"*Wheel of Fortune*, huh? I'm more of a *Price is Right* kinda guy."

"Really?" She laughs. "I figured this would be right up your alley with words and all, Mr. Big-Shot Scrabble Guy."

"I am actually surprisingly good at Scrabble," I say in a monotone voice, fully acknowledging that it comes as a shock that I'm great with words. "I'm smarter than you think. I'm not just a pretty face, sweetheart."

"Didn't think you were, don't worry." She presses pause on the remote and stands up. "I'm gonna grab a snack. You want something?"

I shrug. "Chips and salsa?" I throw a wink her way, wondering if she'll remember our drunken late-night snack—and then the kiss that came after that snack.

"How about some homemade ice cream that your mommy made you?" Her words bring me right back down to reality.

She grabs the container of vanilla ice cream out of the freezer and scoops some into two bowls. She takes the sprinkles out of the drawer and shakes some onto each, then slides a spoon into each bowl.

"What if I didn't want sprinkles?" I eye the multi-colored

bits of candy that are completely covering the ice cream she just handed me. "A little heavy-handed with them, don't ya think?"

"Who doesn't like sprinkles?" she asks incredulously, sliding to sit just slightly closer to me than before. It's moments like these that I've been grasping and holding onto. Moments where she does something that makes me wonder if she's feeling a pull toward me, even just a fraction as much as the one I feel toward her.

It's in the sitting extra close on the couch, the lingering eye contact that lasts just a touch longer than normal, and the way she makes a point to touch me when it's absolutely not necessary, like lightly grasping my forearm when she's squeezing behind me in the tight space of the kitchen.

It's torture, for sure, given I can't have her, but it's not really something I can control at this point. I'll take any hint of affection she'll give me—no matter how small.

"They're just too sweet. A couple is fine, but too much just overpowers the ice cream," I say while using the back of my spoon to move some sprinkles off the top.

"Wow. I didn't know you were so opinionated about sprinkles. Why do you have them in your drawer, then?" She brings a spoon to her mouth but pauses before taking a bite. "Wait, let me guess. Your mom?"

I chuckle. "I think one of my sisters stuck them in there. My whole family insisted on helping me get settled when I moved and stocking the drawers and cabinets with any and everything I might potentially need someday was high on their list—whether I like the item or not. That's my family for you. But you know that already," I say, fully enjoying the fact that she knows about the inner workings of my family.

The clank of her spoon against the bowl draws my head in her direction. She licks the corner of her mouth with her tongue, and the hair on the back of my neck stands straight up. Air gets caught in my throat, and suddenly, I can't breathe.

You would think I would be used to the way my body involuntarily reacts to her by now, but it stops me in my tracks every time. I get lost for a few moments, staring at her lips, remembering how they taste, how they feel pressed against mine, then I lift my gaze higher to connect with her emerald eyes staring back at me. They're piercing mine with an intensity that more than confirms she was thinking about the same thing.

Like hell if I'm gonna be the one to look away first. I get lost in time for a moment when I swear she leans in slightly, and my heart starts racing.

"Hey," John's voice breaks us out of our trance as he comes inside and knocks on the door in one fluid movement. I clear my throat, and Paige jumps, shifting her body farther away from mine.

John gives us a skeptical look and then comes barging in, making me regret that we have the kind of friendship where he just lets himself in. He heads to the fridge to grab a beer and then sits on the chair next to the couch.

"Hey, John," Paige says, her voice slightly unsteady.

"What's up, man?" I ask, still trying to shift my thoughts away from Paige. "We can't game tonight. She already claimed the TV."

He takes a long swig, sets the bottle on the table, and looks at us. "I want to talk to you guys."

"Okay," I say cautiously.

"Where's Mia?" Paige sounds concerned.

"She's with Quinn. They went to pick up dinner. She doesn't know I'm here, so I don't have a lot of time."

"Shut up! Shut up! Shut up!" Paige squeals next to me, placing her bowl of ice cream on the coffee table before clapping her hands together. I look at her in confusion, wondering what the hell she's doing.

"Tell me you're planning to propose! Are you proposing?"

John nods his head with a chuckle. "How did you know?

Yeah, I came to ask you both for help. I needed to come in person instead of calling so I wouldn't leave a trail on my phone that Mia would find."

Paige makes some sort of high-pitched squealing noise while jumping up to run and throw her arms around John. I zero in on his hand that comes to rest between her shoulder blades, jealousy buzzing through me before I remind myself that I'm an adult—an adult who is fully capable of managing his emotions. I clear my throat once again, able to finally tame the jealousy once Paige releases John.

"Congrats, man. That's a big move!" I give him a fist-bump, then settle back into the couch.

"So, what's your plan? When are you going to do it?" Paige asks.

"I'm thinking next weekend. I'd like to propose to her on the beach at sunset and then have you guys all show up behind her to celebrate. I know it's not super original, but I think Mia will love it."

Paige nods her head, pushing her lips together. "She will," she whispers.

"Are you crying?" I ask, putting a hand on her shoulder.

She runs her finger under her eye while shaking her head. "I'm just so happy for her… and you!" She gestures toward John, who responds with a smile.

"Thanks. It'll mean the world to her that you're there. So, if you two can be in charge of inviting and making sure everyone gets there on time, that would be great. I was thinking we should invite Brian, Julie, and Hazel. And Quinn, obviously, but I should be able to find a time to fill her in. And anyone else you think she'd love to have there. Oh, also! Paige, do you think you can FaceTime Mia's parents while it's happening so they can be part of it, too?"

"Absolutely! Good idea," she responds.

"Great, thanks," he says before downing the last drop of beer and standing up. "I should get going before they get back. Thanks for your help on this, guys. It means a lot."

"Of course, man. Happy for you." I give him a good bro hug with a slap on the back, then turn back to the couch while Paige gives him another hug—figured I'd pass on watching this time.

John leaves Paige and me alone once again.

"Oh my gosh, I'm so excited," she breathes.

"It's pretty exciting," I agree. I can't help but think that this only solidifies the fact that Paige will be coming to Hawaii frequently to visit for the foreseeable future. Maybe one of these times, she'll change her mind about me. A guy can only hope.

"Alright, where were we?" I unpause *Wheel of Fortune,* and we get back to eating our ice cream. I don't think I've ever had this much fun just watching TV, and the rest of the night goes by quickly. She rags on me for not knowing what the word is in an appropriate amount of time, and I take it on the chin, stealing occasional glances at her out of the corner of my eye. When I eventually crawl into my bed later, I fixate on the several times I caught her glancing at me, too.

18

———————

PAIGE

In contrast to how I look stumbling out of my room most mornings, I waltz toward the kitchen this morning, fully dressed and ready to go. Usually, my tutoring sessions are in the afternoon, but today, it's scheduled for this morning. Something about an open house at the school this afternoon, so we need to meet before then.

I pull my hair back into a loose braid as I walk, my eyes on Matt the entire time. He's standing by the stove, pushing scrambled eggs back and forth with a spatula—shirtless, of course. I've learned that Matt lives in gray sweatpants and no shirt in the mornings. To be fair, if I had his abs, I would probably do the same. Why cover those gorgeous muscles up? He runs a hand through his dirty-blond hair, scratching lazily at the base of his neck, looking deep in thought.

"Don't stand too close. A burn scar would mess up those

obnoxious abs," I point out, reaching into the fridge for a small bottle of orange juice.

"That would be a real shame, wouldn't it?" His level of seriousness about his appearance always makes me laugh. He slides some eggs onto two plates and sets one in front of me. "You're up early today."

"Yeah, I have to be at the school in an hour, and I feel like walking this morning instead of ordering a ride. Thanks for the eggs." I pull two forks out of the drawer and hand him one.

"Nice morning for a walk," he says in agreement. I can feel his eyes scanning me, and it wakes up the ever-present butterflies that seem to have taken permanent residence in my stomach lately.

"No contacts today?" He shoves a forkful of eggs in his mouth, eyeing the glasses I'm still wearing.

"Nope. One of the kids I'm tutoring wears glasses, and I'm trying to make him feel more comfortable. Thought wearing my glasses today might help." I shrug. I'd do anything if I thought it might make Elliot feel more comfortable with me. I have this unexplained need to try and be there for this boy in any way I can. I'd really like to be one of the few adults in his life that he can count on.

"That's really sweet of you," he says sincerely. "But I gotta say, the glasses are doing nothing to tone down this teacher fantasy I'm trying really hard to ignore."

"Ugh, have I told you lately that you're exhausting?" I place my plate in the sink and reach for my sunglasses before setting them back down, remembering I don't need them—I'm wearing glasses today.

He smirks, totally witnessing and loving how distracted he's making me, then he smiles sweetly. "Not today."

"I'm out," I say, walking to the door. "See ya later!"

"Bye," I hear him call out before I shut the door. I smile to myself as I make my way out of the building and onto the sidewalk next to the parking lot.

Matt truly is one of a kind. I don't think anyone has ever made me laugh as hard as he does, and I find myself getting excited every time I hang out with him, wanting to stay at home and be with him instead of going out, which is completely ridiculous since I came here to paradise to spend time with my best friend. We should be hitting up every tiki bar in sight without a care in the world, spending long relaxing days on the beach. And to be fair, we definitely do that. I've just been finding myself thinking about Matt constantly, wondering what he's doing and when I'll see him next.

The sidewalk threads between neighborhoods with some stretches running right along the entrance of the beach, palm trees scattered sporadically on the way. I take my time, soaking in the sun and letting the warmth engulf me like my very own personal tropical hug. I pass a small farmer's market with two small tables of pineapples, coconuts, and papayas laid out, and I make a mental note to stop on my way back.

After about twenty minutes, the school comes into sight just ahead. I stop in the office to grab my folder of worksheets, and I see Elliot sitting on a chair by the front desk. I wonder how long he's been waiting there.

"Hey, Elliot!" I smile at him.

He looks up, noticing me for the first time. "Hi, Miss C.," he says in his standard quiet whisper. I watch him study me, focusing on my glasses, and he smiles—I'm hoping because maybe he understands the point of me wearing them.

I smile back, walking over to his chair and crouching down to his level.

"I'm happy to see you today," I tell him, looking him in the eyes. "Guess what I dreamt about last night?"

He shrugs, a smile threatening to emerge on his face.

"Dragons! I tell ya, it's all these books we're reading that's making me have crazy dreams!"

A hint of a giggle escapes his throat, and it sends a rush of happiness through me.

"Should we head to the library?" I ask him. After he nods, we head down the hall and start our work for the day.

The next couple hours are spent reading, practicing our spelling, and working on a few math problems. Time passes quickly, and it isn't until I get a text notification on my phone that I look down and see that our time is up.

Matt: Meet me outside.

I stare at the text in confusion.

Paige: Outside where?

Matt: I'm outside the school.

Huh? What's he doing here?

Paige: Be out in a min.

I walk the kids back to the office, and after telling them how proud I am of their work today, I head out the front doors, where I see Matt. He's in a white T-shirt, his hands tucked in the pockets of black basketball shorts, kicking at the ground with his tennis shoes.

"Hey! What are you doing here?" I ask him, skipping down the steps.

He shrugs. "Just thought I'd keep you company on the walk home."

Something flutters in my stomach, and I smile back at him.

"You did, huh?" I fall into step next to him as we start walking side by side.

"I was bored...literally couldn't think of anything else to do," he teases.

"Uh-huh, sure." I tap him with my elbow. "Well, thanks. It's nice to have company."

Our eyes meet, and I have a hard time tearing them away. I do, but only when I have to move behind him to let a few bikers pass by. I take the opportunity to blow out a breath and calm myself down. It's absolutely silly that he gets me all flustered, and I'm not used to a guy affecting me this way.

Pull it together, Paige.

"How did tutoring go?"

"Really great. I'm really glad I stumbled on this opportunity while I'm here—makes me feel useful," I say.

He shoots me a sideways smile.

"Oh, I totally want to stop here and get some pineapple. Do you mind? It looks so good." I stop at the produce stand to pick up and inspect the fruit.

"Go for it. It's some of the best you'll find," he says, perusing the selection and then picking up a couple coconuts. "Would I even be a gentleman if I didn't make sure you stayed hydrated in this heat? Coconut water?" He holds them up and raises his eyebrows in anticipation.

I laugh. "Sure, that sounds great, actually." Matt pays for my pineapple as well as two coconuts. The vendor sticks a straw in each of them before handing them to us.

"Cheers." Matt clinks his coconut with mine, and I take a sip as we head back on our way.

"Cheers. Oh wow, that's good," I say, sipping from the straw, letting the refreshing liquid coat my throat.

We walk the rest of the way, drinking our coconut water, chatting about our mornings. Each step we take, we seem to gravitate closer to each other, like there's an invisible string drawing us together. I'm not sure if he's the one moving my way or if it's me inching closer to him, but by the time we make it to the apartment building, our arms are practically pushing against each other. We toss our coconuts in the garbage before heading inside.

Matt opens the door for me, and I start walking up the flight of stairs, sensing him close behind, practically hovering over my shoulder. When we get to our door, I set the pineapple on the small table in the hallway and pull the key out of my pocket.

I'm hyper-aware that Matt is just inches behind me, his head hanging down like it's taking everything in him to not be even closer. My heart starts beating faster, and a tingle runs down my arm at the faintest draft of his breath on my neck.

I unlock the door, but something inside me stops my hand from opening it. As if my body has a mind of its own, I slowly turn around until I'm staring directly at his chest, and I wonder if his heart is racing as much as mine. I look up to find his eyes burning into mine, a slightly pained expression on his face.

"What are you doing?" he asks in a slow, gruff voice.

Good question.

It's been hard enough to resist him lately in our daily interactions, but when he's this close, it's damn near impossible. Confusion consumes my mind as I try to remind myself of the pros and cons of kissing him, of why I've been resisting him this long.

"I'm not sure," I tell him honestly.

He scans my face and bites his lower lip. "Paige…" He comes just an inch closer, his muscled frame overshadowing mine, and my breath catches in my throat. "You turned me down once already," he says in a slow, deep voice. He comes just slightly closer, bringing his head down, so it's next to mine, and leans into my ear.

"I'm not gonna be the one to make the first move," he breathes into my ear, sending a shiver straight down my spine.

He pulls back slightly to connect his eyes with mine, and my brain starts going crazy.

How would this end? Would it make everything awkward? Would it completely ruin our friendship?

"Screw it," I breathe out a mere second before connecting my lips with his, sliding my arms around his waist to pull him closer. He doesn't hesitate, and he pushes his fingers into my hair as his hands cradle both sides of my jaw. He pushes his lower body against mine until my back is flat against the door, his hips pinning mine in place.

I scrape my fingertips up his back a few inches, and he responds by kissing me deeper. Every nerve ending in my body is bursting awake with each second that passes. One of his hands moves to the doorknob behind me, and he pushes it open, gently moving us along with it. He kicks it closed behind him, and we stumble to the couch.

Gently pushing him down, so he's lying flat on his back, I lower myself on top of him, one leg resting between his, never once breaking the kiss.

One of his hands slides down to cup my butt over my jean shorts while the other runs up the center of my back. I hear my phone ringing and mentally curse whoever's calling, but then I remember that Mia and I have lunch plans.

Ugh.

I break the kiss and lean down to plant a kiss just below his ear, then another on his collarbone, not quite able to stop touching him yet.

"I have to get that," I whisper against the skin of his chest, my phone ringing for the second time.

"Uh-uh," he grunts, pulling me back up to his lips. I indulge him with one more kiss, then push myself off his chest to lift myself up. I climb all the way off of him, his hand grabbing mine on the way. I find his fiery eyes piercing mine, a somewhat dazed expression on his face. I'm torn between wanting to answer my phone and wanting to crawl back on top of him and stay there the rest of the day.

"I have to meet Mia for lunch," I say, slowly running my thumb across his knuckles. He nods, pulling his hand away so he can shift himself up to sit on the couch, eyes never leaving mine.

"Just talk to me for a second?" he asks, his eyes locking with mine.

I nod, shoot Mia a quick text, and slowly drop down to sit next to him, trying my best to ignore the strong desire to push him back down.

"We just made out, and now you want to talk about our feelings? Aren't you cute," I tease him, a smile forming on my lips.

"Yup. Not even ashamed to admit it, either." His confidence and steady voice are impressive, like we didn't just tilt our entire friendship on its axis.

"I just want to check in, make sure you're good. You had your reasons for not getting involved with me, and I respect those. What changed your mind? Do you need to think about this some more?"

"Matt, when I said, 'Screw it,' and kissed you, that was me thinking about it and choosing to kiss you," I say with a smile, then let out a sigh. "Listen, I still don't know if this is a good idea, but clearly, there's something between us that's too hard to ignore anymore," I say with a shrug. "Let's just try and keep it casual while I'm here. See how it goes."

He nods his head slowly. "I can do that. I can't promise you're not gonna fall in love with me, though—that happens a lot," he teases. I roll my eyes and plant a kiss on his cheek as I stand up, patting his leg.

"I'll try my hardest not to," I say with a smile.

"Hey." He stops me before I get too far. "Can I take you on a date tonight? Totally casual, of course."

A grin spreads across my face, and excitement surges through me.

"Sure."

His smile matches mine, and he pushes himself off the couch. "Great. I'm gonna go surf for a while. I'll text you details." He puts his hand on my shoulder and lets it slide down across my lower back as he moves past me.

I nod, watching him head for the door. He opens it, grabs the pineapple from the table in the hall, and tosses it to me.

"See ya later." He winks and closes the door.

I blow out a breath, sinking back down on the couch, processing what just happened. I roll the pineapple in my hands while replaying the last few minutes, and I can't help the butterflies that flutter in my stomach. Ugh, why does he have to be so good-looking? And charming? And funny? And apparently respectful? He's everything I've been searching for in a guy, and it just figures I'd find him living all the way in Hawaii.

I eventually get up, make a plan with Mia to meet at the local poke shop in town, and check the mirror to fix myself up. She's going to have a field day with this.

19

MATT

"You ready?" I ask later that evening as Paige saunters into the kitchen, looking absolutely stunning. She pulls her curled hair over to one shoulder, then pulls on the strap of what I've learned from my sisters is a mustard-yellow romper that perfectly shows off her long, tan legs.

Damn.

She shrugs, looking somewhat shy, which is unsettling. I've never known her to be anything except the complete embodiment of confidence. Her uneasiness is surprising, and I don't like that she might be feeling even the tiniest bit uncomfortable—especially with me.

"Do I look okay? You didn't tell me what we're doing, so I had no idea what to dress for."

I can't stop my feet as they move toward her. I stop when my body is just inches from hers, my face hovering over hers as she looks up at me.

"You look absolutely gorgeous," I say slowly, which elicits a smirk.

"Thank you," she says sincerely. Her eyes scan mine, and I can almost feel the hesitation leave her body. Her eyes dance with playfulness as her mouth lifts up in an even bigger grin.

"Okay. Take me on a date," she demands, moving around me to grab her purse on the counter, which she swings over her shoulder, cross-body style.

"Yes, ma'am."

We leave the apartment and step out into the humid evening air.

"You're really not gonna tell me where we're going?" she asks, moving through the front door I've held open for her.

"Nope."

"You're kinda big on surprises, aren't you?" she asks, chuckling to herself.

"Life's more fun when you don't know what to expect." I reclaim my spot by her side, and I gesture toward the sidewalk that leads to the beach. "My dad always used to surprise my mom when we were growing up. He would plan special dates or surprise her with flowers or some other gift that made him think of her. This way." I point to the left once we've made it all the way to the beach, then shrug. "I like planning stuff 'cause it shows you put an effort into it. I like thinking about the person I'm with and what would make them happy. I guess I get it from my dad."

"How come I never see your dad stop by the apartment?" She looks up at me as we walk.

"He doesn't come by a lot. He calls me almost every day to check in, and we have a great relationship, but I mostly see him just at the occasional family dinner. He's a financial analyst here in town, and he's very career-driven, so his work takes up a lot of his time." I glance over at her and see sympathy written all over her face.

"It's all good," I chuckle. "He's always made an effort to be a great businessman, but not at the expense of being a great dad. He did a great job balancing the two, and we're all adults now, living our own lives, so he doesn't need to be around as much. He was around more when we were younger."

"I'm glad." She shoots me a smile. I take the opportunity to reach out and thread my fingers with hers, the connection enticing me to open up to her even more.

"Sometimes, I worry that I don't make him proud enough, don't live up to his expectations. I'm sure he would prefer it if I was working some fancy corporate job. That's another reason I want this promotion so bad. There's a big difference in saying, 'My son's a bar manager,' versus just a bartender, you know?"

"Lead bartender," she corrects me. "I see where you're coming from, but for the record, I think your dad is proud of you already. Just the way you are. If he's anything like the rest of your family, I'm sure he loves just as strongly and unconditionally as the rest of them. You know what?" Her eyes get wide. "I just realized that they are totally where you get your confidence from. I blame your family for molding you into the most arrogant, cocky guy who believes he's God's gift to the world," she laughs.

"Hey!" I laugh, pretending to be offended, then lift my shoulders in a shrug. "You're probably right."

She squeezes my hand, letting me know she's just messing with me. We take our sandals off and gravitate closer to the ocean, letting the waves wash over our feet as we walk.

"Enough about me...what about you? Are you close with your family?" I ask.

"I am." The way her face lights up shows how highly she thinks of them. "It's kind of hard to not be close when you move around so much, you know? My brother, Caleb, was my best friend, even though he's six years younger. All we had was each other, really. Friends came and went just as quickly as our homes did. It wasn't until we settled down in Minnesota that we were able to build quality relationships with other people. We never lost our family connection, though. I know that isn't the same for everybody, so we're definitely lucky."

"I love that your family is so close. Is Caleb overprotective like I am with my sisters? Would he like me or hate me?" I ask.

"Oh, he'd hate you for sure." She didn't hesitate, and I let out a laugh. "He's hated most guys I've gone out with, and he definitely doesn't warm to arrogant ones easily." She smiles. "He'd get used to you, though, and grow to like you."

"Kinda like you did?"

"Eh, jury's still out on whether or not I like you," she teases.

"It's only a matter of time. Trust me." I shoot her a wink.

"Hey, do you want me to kick your butt real quick before we keep going?" I motion to the same volleyball nets we played on as we pass by.

She snorts. "If I recall correctly, it was my team that beat your team."

"That's not how I remember it. We might need a rematch."

"Deal."

We continue walking, her hand fit snugly into mine, slowing down our pace as we dodge seashells and rocks. I see Marty's Beach Bar up ahead and steer Paige out of the water.

"Okay, every good date has phases, right? In my book, at least, they're a necessity," I tell her, walking us in the direction of the bar. "We've officially arrived at phase one. A pre-dinner refreshment at Marty's." I stretch my arm out in front of me to showcase the old sun-faded building.

"Ooh, I love Marty's! Nice job on phase one." She gives me a high-five.

I hold open the door, and my heart skips a beat at the strawberry-vanilla scent of her perfume that just subtly washes over me. She leads the way to the bar, where she pulls a stool back to slide onto. I claim the stool next to her, sliding it slightly closer to her as I sit.

"Well, look what the cat dragged in." Marty shuffles over to us.

"Hi, Marty!" Paige says.

"Paige, how are you, sweetie?" Marty asks, placing two cocktail napkins down.

"Pretty good," she says sweetly with a smile.

"What can I get ya?"

"I'll have a Mai Tai, please," Paige says.

"Gold Cliff for me, please," I chime in.

"You got it." Marty gets to work grabbing our drinks.

"How are things going here?" I ask and watch him suck a deep breath in.

"Holding steady. I got a water leak out down the hall by the restroom. Damn pipe rotted and gave out. Water everywhere. I shut the water off until I can get around to fixing it."

"I can help you with that," I offer. "I don't work till tomorrow night, so I'll swing by in the morning to take a look."

"Oh, you don't have to bother with that. I can handle it." He waves me off, not wanting to accept help.

"It's really no problem, Marty. I'd be happy to help," I insist.

"No, thank you," he says sternly. "Now, drink up." He places our drinks on the napkins and shuffles over to where a group of people just sat down at a high-top.

"You're still gonna show up tomorrow, aren't you?" Paige asks, bringing her Mai Tai to her mouth.

"Yup." I've known Marty long enough to know that he doesn't like accepting help from anyone, as if it would be a direct insult to his pride. But I also know that he's got a lot on his hands with this place, and it wouldn't feel right if I didn't help out if I could.

"Alright, phase one also must include quality conversation," I say.

"Oh, it does, does it?" She raises her eyebrows. "What do you wanna talk about?" She shifts her body so she's angled toward me, ready for any topic.

"Have you always wanted to be a teacher?"

She doesn't have to think long before answering. "Pretty much. I used to play school and pretend Caleb was my student all the time growing up. That was my favorite game. And then, when I got older, I babysat a lot. I've just always loved kids and teaching. I don't remember ever wanting to be anything else."

"That's awesome."

"Okay, I have a question." She clears her throat after a minute of comfortable silence.

"Shoot."

"What's something on your bucket list?"

"My bucket list?"

"Yeah, something you want to do in your life before you die?"

"Hmm, good question." I think for a second. "I've always wanted to dive the Great Barrier Reef. That's pretty high up on my bucket list. That and maybe enjoy a cigar in Cuba. That'd be pretty badass."

She laughs. "Those are some pretty good ones!"

"What about you?"

"I've always wanted to go in the Blue Lagoon in Iceland. Oh, and Mia and I have always wanted to visit a winery in every U.S. state. So far, we've made it to just four, so we have a ways to go." She laughs, the dim light making the green in her eyes sparkle. I get lost in them for a minute, letting a warmth sweep over me that has nothing to do with the lack of air conditioning in this place.

"Alright, ready for the next phase?" I ask her.

She downs the last sip of her drink and smiles.

"Bring it on."

I throw enough cash on the bar to cover our drinks and a generous tip.

"See ya tomorrow, Marty!" I call.

"I better not, Matt! Bye, Paige. Make sure he's treating you with respect now, alright?"

"Yes, sir," she says.

We make it back into the sand, and I steer us to the left again, continuing in the same direction we were headed. I don't waste more than five seconds before I grab her hand again—a move she clearly appreciates, judging by the smile on her face.

We walk for about a quarter mile, making small talk the whole way, until the faint sounds of chanting music becomes louder and louder. The sun is just starting to set as we stumble upon my next location.

"Welcome to phase two," I tell her. "A traditional Hawaiian luau."

20

PAIGE

"I signed you up to dance," I tell Matt, sliding into the folding chair next to him, moving my plate of delicious half-eaten poi and kalua pork that we ate to the side. I have to almost yell it to be heard over the beating of the drums that are so loud it's vibrating in my ears.

He chokes on his last bite of food, his eyes going wide in alarm. "You what?"

I can hardly suppress laughter as it bubbles up my throat. "I saw a sign-up sheet for hula dancers on my way back from the bathroom. Thought that would be something you would enjoy. You'll join them onstage when they call for volunteers. It's so nice of you to participate." I pat him on the back and watch as his expression slowly shifts from shock to resolve.

"You think I don't know how to hula?" He moves closer, pinning me with a look. "I've lived here since I was in fourth grade. I've done it all, honey. Just wait till you see me."

"Oh, good. You'll be right at home up there, then."

He's barely able to contain the grin spreading on his face before saying, "And will you be joining me?"

I shrug, not doing a very good job at keeping a straight face despite my efforts. "I'll pass this round. You seem to love being the center of attention. I'm just helping you shine, hot stuff."

His eyes dance with amusement as we hear a voice on the speakers, booming to be heard over the music.

"Aloha! I hope you all had a chance to grab some food— lomi salmon, poi, laulau, kalua pig, and poke—all kinds of amazing food to feast on! Please help yourself! At this time, I'd like to welcome up to the stage anyone who has volunteered to hula with our dancers. Make your way to the right of the stage, please. Anyone is welcome!"

"Oh, you're up, Matthew!" I pat his leg a few times in faux excitement. He looks resigned, shaking his head slowly. I should really be ashamed at how much enjoyment I get from messing with him, but it's just too much fun—and way too easy.

He comes to the back of my chair, placing both hands on either side of it. I can feel his breath on my neck as he lowers his mouth to my ear, sending a shiver straight down my spine before he even says a word.

"Watch and learn, sweetheart," his voice low and quiet, so only I can hear him. My voice catches in my throat, and I can't choke out any snarky comments before he's up on the stage, finding his place right in the middle of the dancers.

He's joined by a few couples and several children who fill in the empty spaces on stage. I watch in amusement as a new song starts, and Matt eats up the attention, expertly moving his hips and keeping up with the dancers. He finds me in the crowd every few minutes and either winks or grins suggestively, both of which make me laugh.

I let out a loud catcall when the music pauses, and the volunteers exit the stage. I watch as Matt saunters back to the table, fist-bumping a few people on the way, relishing the attention in a way that only people who love the spotlight do.

"Did ya like that?" he asks, sliding into his seat.

"Not too bad for a guy with no rhythm," I tease.

"Oh, whatever. You couldn't peel your eyes off of me. I saw you admiring the show." His brows wiggle.

The music starts thumping loudly again as several fire dancers take the stage. I'm thoroughly impressed as I watch them fling their fire-lit wooden swords up into the air. They twirl and dance around each other, taking up every inch of space on the stage.

"So you said you've done it all. Can you do that, too?" I ask, gesturing to the dancers.

"That I leave to the professionals," he laughs.

"So, most of the people here are guests of the resort, right?" I peer around at the crowded tables, jam-packed with people. I have to imagine this is a popular attraction for many people.

"Yup, the hotel puts on a traditional luau like this on the beach for the guests about once a week, I'd say. It's pretty touristy, but I thought it was something you should experience at least once." His eyes connect with mine, and I can't bring myself to look away. Apparently, he can't either because we stay lost in each other's eyes, the hum of electricity between us gradually getting stronger as the music continues pounding.

"Should we head out?" His gravelly voice cuts through the humid air, barely loud enough to hear.

I nod slowly, only breaking my eyes from him when he offers his hand to help me up. His fingers lace through mine, and he leads us back in the direction we came, his hand holding mine just slightly tighter than before.

The drum of the music eventually starts fading out as we walk on the dark beach, the only light coming from the sporadic bars and houses we pass by, barely enough to see more than a couple feet in front of us at a time.

"So…getting back to our quality conversation…" He turns his head in my direction, then down to where our feet are leaving imprints in the sand. "What do you like the most about Minnesota?"

I smile, appreciating his efforts to get to know me. "Oh gosh, that's a hard question. What's not to love?" I grasp onto his hand tighter as he gently pulls me around a large seashell jutting from the sand. "I guess aside from the obvious—like my friends and family being there—there's just so much to do. In the winter, I do a lot of skiing and snowmobiling. And then, since I have the summers off, I pretty much spend it all outside, most often at friends' cabins, boating, and swimming. We've got some great hiking and bike trails. Oh, and my family and I go up to the Superior National Forest every year to kayak and camp in the Boundary Waters."

"I love it. Sounds like a great place. Maybe I'll visit there someday." I look up to catch a smile tugging at the corner of his mouth.

"So," he changes the subject, "on any given Saturday morning, what is Paige Campbell doing?"

I think it over for a second. "If it's summer break, probably sleeping in and getting ready to go to an outdoor patio for brunch with either my mom or some friends."

He nods his head in approval.

"What about you?" I ask. "What's your favorite thing about living here? I almost feel silly asking that. I should just ask what you don't like, if anything."

He chuckles. "It is pretty amazing, I'll give you that. Can't beat the weather, and being just a stone's throw away from the beach and surfing is pretty much all I need in life." He glances down at the sand.

"Although, I'm starting to think of one thing that's a negative against Hawaii." He sweeps his eyes sideways briefly to meet mine.

"What's that?" I ask.

"It's not where you live."

I let his answer warm my chest as I squeeze his hand in response, feeling suddenly shy and out of words.

We walk a few more steps in silence. The waves crashing onto shore are the only visible part of the ocean in the darkness as we walk.

"You really pulled out all the stops on our date tonight," I laugh. "I thought this was supposed to be casual."

He shrugs nonchalantly. "I don't really do casual, Paige, especially when it comes to something I really like." He says it so casually, like his words aren't causing everything inside me to be shaken up and jumbled.

I manage a smile and clear my throat.

"So we've had two phases. Do I dare ask if there's a phase three on this date?" I ask.

"Phase three is usually the end of the date. Its contents and activities can vary, but the one thing it must always include is a goodnight kiss. Speaking of..." he says, mischief laced in his voice.

"Is that right?" I grin.

He slows our pace, moving so his body comes right in front of mine, stopping me in my tracks.

"Oh, is this happening now?" I laugh. "I thought the goodnight kiss was for when we say goodnight."

He smiles, using his free hand to grab my waist and pull me closer until there's no space between us. The light from a tiki bar half a mile away slightly illuminates his face, just enough so I can still see the blue of his eyes. His other hand untangles from mine to rest on my lower back, and I bring my hands up to his neck.

"I can't go another second without kissing you," he whispers, his heated stare taking my breath away. I stay glued to his eyes until he leans forward and gently presses his lips to mine. If our kiss earlier today was heated and hungry, this one is the opposite. Soft, tender, and safe. He moves his lips slowly against mine like he's savoring every single second. Here in the dark, the sound of waves crashing onto shore right next to us, I lean into Matt's kiss, pressing myself into him.

I curl my fingers and lightly scratch the back of his neck, where I've watched him scratch with his own fingers countless times. I feel a hum vibrate from the back of his throat, his hands sliding up my back. I slide my hands slowly down the sides of his neck, continuing down against the well-defined muscle of his stomach, bringing them to rest on the sides of his hips. At the same time, his hands come up to push through my hair, stopping at the top of my neck.

Eventually, he breaks contact and smiles sweetly, eyes glazed over, wrapping his arms around me in a hug.

It's in this moment, my arms wrapped tightly around his waist, that I feel myself falling a little harder for Matt. Another tiny piece of my heart softens, joining the other tiny pieces that have gradually softened over the past few days, leaving just my mind to grapple with the realistic questions I should be asking myself…but feeling way too giddy to want to listen to it.

21

MATT

"Am I too late?" I whisper in Paige's ear, squeezing between her and Brian. My fingers find and thumb the material of her blue sundress around her waist. Julie, Hazel, Quinn, and a few people from Mia's work are gathered around us, an arching *Congrats* balloon tied to two palm trees over our heads. I'm the last to arrive at the beach—though not by choice. It's been a day. I attempt to shake off my grumpy mood so I can focus on this big moment for John and Mia.

"You're just in time. Oh my gosh," Paige breathes next to me as she wipes a tear from her eye. We watch from a distance as John drops down to one knee, the ocean waves crashing onto shore just a few feet away from where they're standing. The sunset behind them creates a stunning backdrop for the proposal, and Quinn snaps several pictures with her phone.

Mia jumps into his arms less than a second later, knocking

him over before he even has a chance to pull the ring box out of his pocket.

A laugh escapes my throat as we watch them sprawled out on the sand, Mia peppering kisses all over his face. I take a deep breath for what feels like the first time all day. Their happiness is contagious, even from all the way over here.

"Ahh!" Quinn squeals next to Paige, grabbing onto her arm. They jump up and down with giddiness.

"Hey! We're getting dizzy over here!" Mia's parents laugh from the FaceTime video on Paige's phone.

"Sorry!" she says, straightening their view.

John points in our direction, and a surprised Mia starts rushing our way. Hazel breaks away from Julie, running into Mia's arms, the rest of us following quickly behind.

"Congrats, man!" I shake John's hand before pulling him in for a hug. Paige and Mia connect in a hug, and I'm surprised either of them can breathe with how tight they're squeezing each other. I watch in amusement as tears stream down both of their faces, feeling a twinge of jealousy toward John that he has his life so perfectly figured out. What I wouldn't give to have the same.

"I still don't understand the concept of committing to one person for the rest of your life," Quinn says, throwing her arms around John. "But if you're gonna do it, I'm glad you chose Mia."

"You're not a fan of getting married? What's wrong? Scared of commitment?" I ask Quinn in surprise. She's a spontaneous, fly-by-the-seat-of-your-pants kinda girl, but I assumed she'd want to settle down one day.

"Eh, I just think it's boring! Why tie yourself down? No offense, John. I'm very happy for you and Mia!" She giggles, then reaches for the cooler to pop open some champagne.

"What about you, Matt? A ladies' man like you? Will you ever settle down?"

"Of course," I reply. I've always wanted to get married and settle down, create my own family like I had growing up. That's never been a question.

"And give up all your doting fans? God bless the woman who decides to marry you," she teases.

I roll my eyes, too exhausted to think of a decent rebuttal.

"You know I'm just messing with you." Quinn hands me a cup of champagne and a slap on the shoulder. She's lucky she's like another sister to me. I can easily let her words roll right off me.

Mia finally loosens her grip on Paige, and John joins her as she takes Paige's phone and steps off to the side to talk to her parents.

"You alright?" I ask Paige, throwing my arm around her, stifling a laugh that threatens to burst out. She's just so adorable when she's emotional.

She sniffles, wiping at her eyes. "I'm just so happy for them, you know? If anyone deserves to be happy, it's those two."

"Come here." With a chuckle, I wrap her in my arms, feeling the same buzz of energy building that I feel every time I touch her. Letting her grip me tighter, I run my hand down her bare arm that's wrapped around me. I can't help it. I just can't get enough of it. Of her.

She smiles up at me, squeezing tighter for a beat before releasing me completely and rejoining Mia.

"Thanks for your help with all this, man," John says to me, taking a sip of champagne.

"Absolutely. It turned out great…and good choice finally taking my advice on incorporating phases for the big event. Have fun with phase two." I wiggle my eyebrows suggestively. Phase one was obviously the surprise proposal with a few significant people there to celebrate. John planned a nice romantic picnic on the beach for just them for phase two.

"I didn't. It's all one event for me. You're the one who keeps referring to it in phases," he says dryly.

I shrug, unbothered. If he doesn't want to acknowledge and appreciate the genius of phases, that's on him.

After a toast and another round of congratulations, John and Mia head off down the beach toward their picnic. The rest of us pick up any remaining cups and take down the balloons, handing them off to Hazel to take home.

"Bye, Hazel! See you soon!" Paige calls to her and Julie as they carry the balloons back to Julie's car.

"I'm outta here, too," Quinn says. "I'll see you guys later!" She looks back and forth between Paige and me a few times in a not-so-subtle way, then grins and heads off the beach.

"How about some ice cream to top off that champagne?" I ask Paige, wanting to spend some more time with her. Our date to the luau was a few days ago, and we've both been pretty busy since then—although she's been in my thoughts every single second since. "There's an ice cream cart just down the beach a little way."

Her eyes perk up. "I'd love that."

"How did it go keeping Mia occupied this morning?" I ask, not hesitating to thread my fingers through hers as we walk.

She snorts. "It was harder than I thought it was going to be. She kept trying to call John and meet up with him. I had to distract her with shopping and a papaya-banana smoothie from Julie's."

I chuckle, pointing to the white-trimmed cart under the shade of a palm tree with a sign that says 'Sunburst Scoops' on top.

"Hey, Matt!" Addie says from behind the counter. They know me well here. I take Lily on an ice cream date every couple weeks. This is her favorite place to come, so we usually end up here before meeting Ava and my mom at the nearby park just off the beach.

"Hey, Addie. This is Paige."

"Nice to meet you, Paige. I'm not used to seeing him with another grown-up," she laughs. "What can I get you guys?"

"I'll have a small cup of strawberry ice cream, please," Paige answers.

"Make that two," I chime in.

"Extra sprinkles on both, please," she blurts out with a grin.

I just shake my head and pay for the ice cream without bothering to decline the sprinkles. I'll suck it up and eat whatever she wants me to eat. I'm that far gone for her. It's pathetic, I know.

"Bench or beach?" I ask, shoving a spoon in her cup, gesturing at the picnic tables scattered nearby.

"Can we sit by the water?"

"Sure."

We dodge a few beach towels and sandcastles, eventually finding an empty space to sit. The sun is still setting, so there's a little bit of daylight left before it gets dark. After getting situated on the sand, Paige takes her spoon and scrapes at the sprinkles that are completely coating my ice cream.

"Don't worry, I'll eat your sprinkles." She scoops them straight into her mouth while I watch every move she makes. She slides the spoon out upside down. It's official: file *watching Paige eat ice cream* under my list of new favorite things to do.

"So, how was your day? You went in to work after setting up the balloon and coolers, right?" she asks.

I let out a sigh. "Yeah, Mike called me in for a quick meeting."

"Uh-oh, you don't look very happy. What happened?"

"He called me in to give me an update on the manager position."

"Let me guess…Steve's the new manager?" she asks quietly.

"Yup." Hearing it out loud, especially from Paige, stings just as bad as when Mike gave me the news.

"I'm sorry," she says regretfully.

"Nothing I can do about it." I shrug. Not getting the promotion is a real kick to the shins. I'm not sure what direction I'll go from here. I guess I'll stay and keep working my regular shifts, doing the same old bartending duties day in and day out until the next opportunity comes along. Or maybe I should switch things up and actually use my degree. Who knows? It's all up in the air at this point.

She eyes me. "It's okay to be disappointed, you know."

"I prefer to not dwell on the negative stuff. Plus, I respect his decision. He must not have seen me as having manager material, and that's alright. On to something new, I guess."

"Matt, don't be so hard on yourself. If climbing the ranks in the bartending world is what you want to do, then stick with it. Just because this opportunity slipped you by doesn't mean there isn't another. Maybe other bars are hiring? Where's the confidence?" She shoves my arm with her elbow playfully.

"I also got a flat tire on my way back. That's why I was late. Just isn't my day, I guess," I muse.

"Dang, that sucks." She sets her empty ice cream cup on the sand and slides closer to me, wrapping her arms around my arm that's propped up on my knees. "Hopefully, your evening will turn around."

"It already has." I smile and plant a kiss on her temple. She lays her head on my shoulder, and I rest my chin in front of her head, my nose sliding into her hair. The scent of her shampoo fills my senses, overwhelming me in the best way. The gray cloud hanging over my future and career goals dissipates with every second that passes as we sit watching surfers and swimmers out in the water, soaking up the last few minutes of daylight. We stay silent like that for a long time before eventually getting up and walking home.

22

PAIGE

"You look absolutely gorgeous today," Matt's throaty morning voice whispers in my ear behind me as he wraps two strong arms around my middle, resting his chin on top of my shoulder.

"Hmm," is all my pre-coffee brain can muster.

He chuckles against my neck. I fill the space between us, curving my back to fit nicely against his chest. He holds me there for a charged moment that tingles on top of my skin. I momentarily get lost in him, in this cocoon of muscle that's surrounding me, not wanting to move.

"Cereal?" He eventually loosens his grip to reach for two bowls in the cabinet above my head.

"Cheerios, please." I move around him to grab the milk out of the fridge.

"Who likes plain Cheerios, anyway? They're so boring."

"Says the man who doesn't like sprinkles," I retort.

"Not the same." He pours cereal into our bowls—Cheerios for me, Raisin Nut Bran for him—and I top them off with milk.

"Damn, you look good in those shorts," he says as he trails behind me, walking to the table.

I eye him suspiciously. "Why are you buttering me up?"

"I dunno." He shrugs nonchalantly, focusing on his bowl. "Just seemed like a good idea, I guess."

A laugh bursts out of me, followed by an exasperated sigh. He has this annoying yet impressive way of always saying just the right thing to make me laugh. Whether I'm laughing with him or at him is beside the point.

"What are you up to today?" I ask, taking a bite of my deliciously boring cereal.

"I'm gonna swing by Marty's this morning to drop off a few light bulbs I ordered for him. Noticed a few were burnt out last time I was there. Probably see if I can convince him to let me fix a few of the broken floorboards," he says. "Then I work the late shift tonight at the bar."

"It's nice of you to help Marty out. I'm sure he appreciates it, even if he doesn't show it."

He chuckles, "Yeah, he's a stubborn one, that's for sure. What do you have planned?"

"I have to tutor in a little bit, and then Quinn and I are gonna take Mia out for a girls' afternoon to celebrate her engagement. I think we'll hit up one of the resort spas for lomi lomi massages and mimosas."

"Sounds girly." His head nods.

I'm about to make a remark about how I am, in fact, a girl, and so are Mia and Quinn, but I'm interrupted by the front door slowly creeping open. Tori, who has one hand strategically placed over her eyes, pushes the door farther open.

"Is everyone decent? Fully clothed?" she asks.

Well, that answers whether or not Matt told his family about our date. I've been wondering when I could expect a grilling from Matt's family.

"Ha ha," Matt says, unimpressed.

"Come on in, Tori," I say with a laugh.

She drops her hands, shoots us a grin, and joins us at the table. "Just thought I'd drop by and see how things are going for the new lovebirds. The fam wants an update."

Matt doesn't seem in a hurry to contribute to the conversation, so I don't waste any time chiming in.

"Great!" I say. "We were actually just discussing how many kids we want and where we'll live. I'm expecting a proposal any day now."

Matt's eyes bug out of his face as he stares at his cereal mid-bite, and I can't keep a serious face for the life of me.

"I'm just kidding," I say with a laugh, placing my hand on his shoulder.

"Please tell me you're gonna fall in love and be my new sister—"

"Tori," Matt cuts her off. "Ease off, will ya?"

I laugh in amusement at his red face, absolutely loving how flustered he's getting. "It's okay, Matt. It's time the world knows how obsessed you are with me."

"Alright, alright." He pushes his chair back to stand, but not before I catch a glimpse of a smile. He huffs back into the kitchen, and my eyes follow him as he walks, landing on the clock on the stove.

"Oh, shoot! I gotta go," I cry, jumping out of my chair. "I'm late!"

I run to my room to quickly change, grab my keys and run out the door. "See ya later, Tori! Bye, Matthew! I'll miss you every second I'm gone!"

~

"I'm so sorry I'm late!" I barge into the library exactly eleven minutes past when I was supposed to arrive. I had called Principal Murphy on my way to give her a heads up, so she greeted the kids for me and walked them down to the library. I absolutely hate being late, and I'm so annoyed with myself that I let it happen today.

"It's alright! Life happens," she says warmly. I let out the breath I've been holding, relaxing into a chair, until I notice that her arm is around Elliot's chair, leaning toward him in a comforting manner. My chest tightens when I realize it looks like he's been crying.

"Everything alright, buddy?" I ask gently.

When he doesn't respond, Principal Murphy pats him on the back and rises. "See, I told you she was coming. She's here now, okay?" She turns to me and gives me a reassuring smile. "I think we're good now. Have a good session."

She exits the library, leaving me with Ruby and Graham, who are chatting away, and Elliot, who's breaking my heart more and more with every passing second by the look on his face. Betrayal, anger, sadness, and despondency are all somehow clearly visible.

I give Ruby and Graham an assignment to search the library for a book about summer, and they scurry off.

I'm not sure how much time that'll buy me, but hopefully enough. I lean across the table toward Elliot and say softly, "I bet you don't like when people are late, huh?"

He shrugs. "I'm used to it. Everyone's always late," he says in a small voice.

I don't know what hurts more, the fact that nobody in his life cares enough to show up for him on time, or the fact that he sees me as a significant enough person in his life that my absence affects him. He trusted me on some level, and I let him down.

Inconsistency and lack of a routine must be a common theme in his life. I try to imagine what it must be like as a kid to feel like nobody has your back, no clue when or where you might get left behind or forgotten about. The ache in my chest grows stronger as I contemplate what to say.

"Is it hard sometimes…not knowing when someone's gonna show up? Or what you're going to be doing next? How long you might have to wait?"

He gets agitated, growing frustrated with the well of fresh tears in his eyes, trying to blink them away. He shrugs again, crossing his arms over his body.

"I'm sorry I was late today, Elliot," I say, my voice just above a whisper. "I didn't mean to be, but that doesn't make it any less disappointing, I know."

His shoulders rise and fall with a few deep breaths.

"Sometimes I make mistakes or lose track of time. We're all human, and I can't promise you that I'll never make a mistake again, but I can promise you that I would never, ever, ever do anything on purpose to make you feel bad, okay?"

He lifts his gaze to meet my eyes for the first time today, and I can almost see the weight being slowly lifted off his shoulders. Compassion surges through me, and I realize that I'd do anything to make this boy's life easier. I would show up here every single day if I knew that would make him feel more secure in his life.

I may not be able to do a whole lot about the bigger circumstances of his life, but I can sure as hell do the best I can while we're here. My heart warms at the thought of him feeling a connection to me, and I vow to not let him down again during the remainder of my time here.

"Ready to show me how dragons do math?"

The corners of his lips curve up slightly, and he nods. He starts drawing a picture of a dragon, just like I ask him to do at the beginning of every session, and he writes a number above each spike.

"I like how you drew him having seven spikes. If I were to

draw a dragon, I think I'd make it have ten spikes," I say casually.

"What about fifteen?" His face looks notably lighter than just a few minutes ago.

"That would be a lot of spikes!" I laugh.

"Look what I found!" Ruby exclaims, dropping a book on the table. "An Amelia Bedelia book about summer break!"

"Perfect!" I smile at her. Graham joins us with a book about fishing, and we get to work. The rest of our tutoring time flies by quickly, but the pit in my stomach about Elliot feels just as heavy for the rest of the day.

23

PAIGE

Meet me at 10:00 sharp by the front door. Wear comfy clothes. Or workout clothes. Or whatever. M.

The post-it note stuck to my bedroom door the next morning reads. I scratch at my scalp, further tangling the mess of hair, and carry it with me to the kitchen.

"What's this?" I ask Matt, who's leaning over the counter, stuffing a homemade muffin in his mouth.

"We're going out," he mumbles in between bites.

"Where?"

He gulps down some orange juice before responding. "It's a surprise."

I shake my head. "You and your surprises."

"You're stuck with me all day. I already know you don't tutor, and I told Mia to lay off you for today." He comes closer with a smirk. "Today, you're mine."

Butterflies twist in my stomach. I wrap my arms around his

hips, my fingers grazing where his bare back meets his sweatpants. "I like the sound of that."

"Hmm," he hums in agreement, bringing his lips to softly connect with mine.

"How much time do I have?" I ask when he pulls away.

"It's 9:30 now," he says, checking his watch.

"Okay, I need twenty minutes to shower and change quick." Excitement builds as I think of an entire day spent with Matt. It doesn't even matter what we do. I just want to be with him.

"I'll be waiting." He smiles at me.

I make myself a cup of coffee and bring it with me down the hall. Once I shower, I pull on a pair of black running shorts and a gray workout tank. As I'm getting ready, my mind keeps drifting to Elliot. I wonder what he's doing right now and if he's okay. I tutor again tomorrow, so I'll see him soon. I just can't stop myself from worrying. Hopefully, today is an okay day for him. I plan on asking Principal Murphy if I can have Elliot's caseworker's contact info tomorrow. See if she has any suggestions on how to further connect with him. Maybe there's a way that I can meet with him outside of school. I just feel like there has to be something more I can do in the month that I have left here.

After pulling my hair up into a high pony and applying some sunscreen, I join Matt in the kitchen. He's wearing a light-blue T-shirt and gray basketball shorts, bending over to tie his sneakers.

"Ready?" he asks.

"Yup! So, I know you won't tell me where we're going, but will you at least tell me how many phases to expect?" I ask as we make our way down the stairs to the front door.

"Well, we're looking at three phases—two destinations followed by a solid make-out session. That deserves its own phase," he explains with a wink.

"Who says you're getting a make-out session? That's a little presumptuous, isn't it?" I ask with a laugh.

"Hey, it's your call, but I'm pretty good at reading people, and I just don't think you can resist me."

"Uh-huh," I dismiss him as he leads me to the far end of the parking lot.

"Allow me to introduce you to your mode of transportation today." He gestures to two motorized scooters that are parked side by side.

"Scooters?" I ask excitedly. Mia and I have been wanting to rent a couple of these and ride them around the island, but we haven't had a chance to yet. Too many other activities kept trumping scooters, so I'm excited to finally have a chance to ride one.

"Are you down? You're not one of those girls that hates to get her hair messed up, are you?"

"Oh, shut up. I can ride circles around you in this thing." I raise the kickstand with my foot and push off the ground to set the scooter in motion, using the throttle to make a lazy circle around Matt.

"Alright, easy, Andretti. Wait for me," he chuckles.

"Where are we heading?" I ask him as he fastens the helmet he placed on my head.

"Follow me. We'll be going a ways, so just holler if you need a break." With a grin, he takes off, and I follow him out of the parking lot. We head down the bicycle path that lines the beach, carefully threading between people and palm trees.

I maneuver past a woman and her dog on a leash while admiring the scenery. The beach stretches for miles, people scattered everywhere, and I can see a few glass bottom-sightseeing boats way out in the water.

As I ride, I let myself imagine what a future with Matt would look like. I know with certainty that there would be no shortage of laughter and adventures. I could see myself being really happy with him, and that makes this whole thing super confusing. We obviously have chemistry that I have a hard time ignoring, and he makes me want to break down my trust issues and open up with him more than anyone else ever has, but could we make long-distance work? Is it worth it?

Matt makes a hand signal gesturing for me to follow him off the bicycle path and onto the street. We carefully cross and make our way down a side street, behind a row of touristy gift shops. Matt pulls into an open parking spot at the very end, leaving enough room for me to squeeze in next to him.

"Fun, huh?" he asks with a grin, grabbing the handlebars of my scooter and kicking the kickstand out for me.

"So fun!" I agree. He stretches his arm out and offers his hand. I thread my fingers between his, and he gently pulls me toward the corner restaurant with a surfboard sign above that says The Crispy Flipper.

"Phase one: brunch," he says as we walk through the door. A warmth spreads through my chest as my feet slow to a stop.

"You remembered?" I ask, the corner of my mouth lifting up, thinking back to when he asked what I like to do on the weekends. The smile he shoots my way melts me to my core.

"Of course."

The gentle pull of his hand coaxes my feet to move. He pulls a chair out for me at a small table in the back corner. When he lowers himself onto the one next to me, I scoot my chair so I'm slightly closer to him, our knees touching under the table.

Regardless of what our future plans look like, one thing is for certain—I am fully and completely under the spell of Matt's charm. There's no use trying to fight it anymore. He's won. For the rest of my time here, I want to soak up as much of him as I can.

"Aloha!" our waitress greets us, handing us each a menu. "Can I get you started with something to drink?"

I scan the drink menu and settle on a mango mimosa while Matt orders a Bloody Mary.

"What's good here?" I ask him once she walks away.

He shrugs, shaking his head. "No idea. Never been here."

"Really? Why'd you want to come here, then?"

"Grace said it's the best brunch spot on the island," he says nonchalantly.

A little laugh bubbles out of me. "You asked your sister where we should go? You're so cute!" I curl my hand around the outside of his bicep, unable to resist the urge to touch him, even in this small way.

"I know," he deadpans.

"So, what's your favorite thing to get to eat?" He looks over the menu.

"I usually either get an omelet, waffles, or French toast. This apple-cinnamon French toast looks really good. I might get that. Do you know what you want?"

"I think I'll stick with pancakes. No syrup. Just butter."

"Why does that not surprise me," I say with a laugh. "Let me guess—syrup is too sweet?"

"Don't worry about it. Now, don't get too full. Phase two is pretty active. I don't need you puking everywhere and ruining my perfect date record."

"Yes, sir," I chuckle. "What are we doing? Surfing?"

"I told you, it's a surprise." He smirks.

Our waitress brings our drinks, and we order our food and spend the next hour chatting comfortably. When we're sufficiently full-but-not-too-full, Matt pays the bill, and we head back outside.

Instead of reaching for his scooter, he comes to where I'm standing. "You've got a little something… " He points at his lip, then tilts my chin upward before I can question him, and he lightly brushes his lips against mine.

"Got it," he says smugly, proud of himself.

"Smooth moves there, Casanova." I smile as we fasten our helmets and hop on our scooters.

"On to phase two," he says.

We reverse back out onto the side street and hop back on the bicycle path, continuing in the direction we were headed before stopping for brunch. It's a new area of the island I haven't been to yet, so I take in our surroundings as we venture on. It must be a big spot for tourists because people are jam-packed along the sidewalks, and it's heavily populated with gift shops and food trucks.

Eventually, Matt veers off and comes to a stop next to a bike rack. I follow his lead, parking next to him and sliding my helmet off, smoothing my hair back into a low bun. He locks both of the scooters onto the rack, slipping the keys into his pocket.

"Ready?" he asks.

"Ready," I say, grabbing for the hand he's stretched out toward me, and we make our way onto the beach. I slip my sneakers off and carry them in my other hand, letting my toes sink into the sand with each step. Matt leads me toward a hut with a sign that says Wayne's Watersports.

"Phase two: kayaking."

24

MATT

I slide my phone and wallet into the drybag after Paige's belongings. Setting it in the kayak, I put a small cooler with water bottles next to it, then grab our life jackets and hand one to her.

"You've done this before?" Paige asks, clasping the buckles, nervously eyeing the waves crashing onto shore.

"All the time. You're safe with me. Don't worry. I checked the weather. The water should be nice and calm in the bay over there, so I thought we'd head in that direction." I point off in the distance to the right.

"Okay," she says, although not at all convincingly.

Pete, my buddy from high school and the owner of this watersport hut, gives me the go-ahead. I drag the tandem kayak into the water and motion for Paige to hop in the front. She wades into the water and climbs in, grabbing the paddle with two hands. I carefully climb into the back seat, eliciting a squeal from Paige at the rocking motion, and push my paddle into the water to keep us steady.

"Alright, Matt. I'm literally putting my life in your hands right now. I'm very precious cargo. Don't you dare dunk me," she says in a warning tone.

"Paige. I won't let anything happen to you. I kinda like you, if you haven't noticed," I respond.

We glide up and over several waves, our paddles slicing through the crystal-blue water. Kayaking is one of my favorite things to do. It was one of the first things my dad took me to do when we moved here, and we went often growing up, exploring different coves and scoping out the best snorkeling spots. In high school, John, Brian, and I would take kayaks out and race them or occasionally take some ladies out to impress them with our arm strength. Worked like a charm every time.

But having Paige in the kayak with me adds a whole other layer to the experience that I wasn't expecting. I like showing her around, taking her on adventures. I get a rush just being with her, and doing something that I love to do with her makes this the most exhilarating kayak trip I've ever been on—and it's only been five minutes.

"Oh my gosh! A sea turtle!" Paige points into the water just below us. There are three green sea turtles swimming, with some scattered butterflyfish and coralfish swimming around as well. I take a break from paddling so we can watch. Even having lived here most of my life, the natural beauty and sea life here has never lost its magic for me.

"Green sea turtles are considered sacred in Hawaii," I explain. "They're a symbol of longevity, safety, and spiritual energy. Honu is what they're called in Hawaiian. That's what the elementary school is named after."

"Wow," she breathes, watching their every move. I find myself watching her, mesmerized by the look of wonder on her face as she pushes her sunglasses on top of her head. She catches me staring, but I don't look away.

"What?" she laughs.

"Just enjoying the view," I say.

She smirks and rolls her eyes.

"Gosh, it's so pretty," she says, eyeing the landscape back on shore. In front of us is a large mountain filled with lush greenery and a cliff jutting out on the side.

"John and I came cliff-diving here a couple times when we were young and stupid." I motion to the cliff's edge.

"You jumped off that? Wow, you really were stupid."

"Yup. And don't even think about making a joke about how I haven't changed much."

She snorts a laugh. "You said it, not me."

We move on, making a big loop around the bay, stopping every so often to look for sea life and to take a water break.

On one of those water breaks, she twists back to glance at me. "How are you feeling about the whole work situation? Have you decided what you're gonna do?"

"Nah, I'll probably stay at The Toasted Crab for now. It's good money, and I'll keep my eye out for another promotion or opportunity to come up." I'm not super excited about staying at a job where I feel unfulfilled at the end of the day, but I don't have a lot of other options right now. Something else will come along, I'm sure. I'd rather focus on spending time with Paige while she's here. Figuring out my next career move will be a much-needed distraction when Paige eventually goes home in a couple weeks.

We make a big loop around the bay, and after an hour or so, we make it back to shore to return the kayak. I drag it onto the sand and grab our belongings before saying goodbye to Pete.

"Wow, that was amazing!" Paige says, looping her arm in mine as we walk back to our scooters. "It was absolutely perfect."

"I'm glad you enjoyed it. I had fun, too. It's not over yet, though. There's still phase three." I wiggle my eyebrows for effect, which earns me a laugh and a slap on the arm.

After unlocking the scooters, I place a helmet on Paige's head, my body drifting closer to hers automatically. I can't resist the opportunity, so I place my hand on her lower back, gently pulling her to me, and connect my lips to hers.

"One for the road," I explain between kisses.

"I'm all sweaty," she laughs, pushing me off.

"I like Sweaty Paige," I say with a grin, reaching for my scooter. "You ready?" When she nods, we make our way back to the bicycle lane and take our time traveling back to the apartment. After about thirty minutes, we pull into the parking lot.

"Do we have to return these?" Paige asks, kicking out the kickstand.

"Nah, I can return them tomorrow. I know a guy."

"Of course you do."

I reach for her hand as we walk inside and up the stairs. "So, I'm still holding out hope for a solid make-out session, but phase three does actually have a little substance," I say, unlocking the door.

"Oh yeah? What's that?" she asks, a hint of amusement in her voice but also hesitation, like she's bracing herself for what comes next. Can't say I blame her. I keep one hand firmly connected to hers and use the other to grab my phone and pull up a music app.

"I don't have a fancy speaker set up, but this'll do." I press play on "Lover" by Taylor Swift and set the phone on the kitchen table, pulling her closer to me. I pull her arms up around my neck and rest my hands on her hips. "Now, I'm not much of a Swiftie, but I thought there was no better way to end the date than dancing to the same song we first danced to at the bar, even if it's just in the middle of the apartment."

She squeezes the back of my neck and smiles up at me, taking it all in. "You're so thoughtful. It's perfect."

We sway back and forth, keeping a tight grip on each other. Each second that passes makes my heart beat a little faster, and judging by the rise and fall of her chest, I think it's happening for her, too.

Her green eyes lock with mine, and I have a sudden urge to blurt out everything I've been wanting to say for the past couple weeks. Everything I've been trying to keep in. I figure now's as good a time as any.

"Paige," I say quietly.

"Hmm," she hums, eyes still glued to me.

"I've been trying my best to keep this all to myself 'cause I know you want to keep things casual…but I'm surprisingly not that great at being subtle, and I feel like I just need to throw this all out there."

Her brows lift up in anticipation. "Go on," she says.

"You probably don't know this because you're you, but trust me, you light up every single place you go. You know how you see somebody sometimes, and you think, *'Damn, whoever gets to be with that person is one lucky son of a bitch?'* Well, that's you, Paige. And I wanna be that lucky son of a bitch. I wanna be that guy. The one who gets to be your boyfriend. Who takes you on adventures and dates, and plays video games with you, and snuggles on the couch. Who spoils you and makes sure you're well fed. I mean, we already know I can stand the sight of you in the morning," I tease.

She laughs, then grows serious. "Matt—"

"I know you're gonna say that you're going back to Minnesota soon, and I know that. I would never put pressure on you or ask you to stay, especially for something so new. But that doesn't scare me. We can figure it out. Take our best crack at long distance. I haven't even looked at another girl since you've been around, Paige. I only want you."

Her eyes soften, and something in them tells me she agrees with everything I'm saying.

"Okay," she says softly with a smile.

"Okay?" I ask, not at all playing it cool and sounding way too eager.

"Okay," she confirms, a smile tugging at the corner of her mouth.

In true Matt form, I don't know when to shut my mouth, and I continue rambling. "Let's take it one step at a time. We don't have to figure everything out right away. I mean, who knows? If this works out, maybe I'd move to Minnesota. I think I'd like snow—"

She cuts me off by lifting up and pressing her lips to mine. It only takes a brief second to stop my train of thought, and then I kiss her back, squeezing her hips tighter, pulling her as close as I can get her to me. Her hands run up the sides of my neck to rest near my jaw, her touch sending a shiver straight down my spine.

We get lost in the kiss for several minutes until she runs her hands down my neck, coming to a stop at my chest. She gently pushes me until we're moving backward, still connected by our kiss, Taylor's voice getting quieter with each step.

"Where we going?" I murmur.

"Shh." She quiets me by deepening our kiss. We move down the hall until her foot trips on mine, and we stumble into the wall of the hallway, the weight of her body crashing into mine. She giggles against my chest, wrapping her arms around my waist. I chuckle, bringing my arms around her, savoring the feel of her tucked so closely to me.

She lifts her head, resting her chin on my chest, peering up at me. Any trace of laughter slowly disappears from her face, replaced by something more intense. She bites the corner of her lip, and the energy in the air sparks when I lean down to kiss her again. She indulges me, kissing me back until she slowly backs away from me. The only part of our bodies touching is her hand that's gently tugging on mine to follow her. She drops my arm and walks backward.

"Come on," she says, tilting her head toward her bedroom.

I don't waste any time following her with a smirk on my face, grabbing her by the waist and rushing her into her room, slamming the door shut behind us.

25

MATT

Paige's elbow digging into my ribs pulls me from sleep the next morning. One leg is haphazardly lying across my stomach, and her hair is almost completely covering her face.

I hold back a laugh as I turn on my side, scooping her with me as I move, gently pressing against her stomach until her back rests against my torso. I clear the hair off her face and tuck it behind her as she flutters her eyelids, slowly waking up.

"Has anyone ever told you that you're a terrible sleeper?" I whisper in her ear. "Now I know why you look the way you do in the morning."

"Shut up," she murmurs, bringing her arm to rest on top of mine.

I chuckle, burying my face in her hair, letting the memory of last night consume me. Every single cell in my body fires awake at the memories. If I thought I was obsessed with her before, I wholeheartedly crave her now. It's completely overwhelming. I don't know how I'm ever gonna get this girl out of my system.

I won't have to, if I have anything to say about it.

She lazily runs her finger up and down my arm, scratching from my hand to my elbow, leaving a trail of goosebumps in her wake. I can't think of a time when I've felt this much peace. Lying here with my arms around her, I desperately wish she didn't have to leave soon, that we could do this all the time.

"How are you feeling?" I ask, wanting to ensure that she's good and hoping like hell she feels this as much as I do.

She takes a deep breath in and exhales. "That was actually the best night of sleep I've had since being here."

"If that was a good night, I'd hate to see what a restless night is like for you." I tuck my hand under her side, wanting to touch as much of her as I can.

"You don't have to stay here again if you don't want to. Your loss," she teases with a shrug.

"Uh-uh." I squeeze her tighter and whisper gruffly into her hair. "Anywhere you're willing to let me follow you…I'm there. Not even embarrassed at how desperate that makes me sound."

She rolls in my arms, turning herself all the way around until she's tucked just beneath my chin, her top arm wrapping around my back, fingers brushing the spot between my shoulder blades.

"I like when you sound desperate," she murmurs.

With a smile, I kiss the top of her head. "You still alright with giving this a shot?"

She looks up at me and nods slowly, a hint of a smile playing on her lips. "I really am," she says sincerely.

"You won't regret it," I promise. I get lost in her eyes, then ask, after a short pause, "Can I ask you a question?"

"Shoot," she whispers, her eyes still holding mine.

"Why is there a picture of Bradley Cooper on your nightstand?"

A laugh bursts out of her mouth, and she presses her forehead against my chest.

"Should I be worried? Do I have competition?" I tease her with a laugh.

"Don't you worry about Bradley. He goes where I go. We're kind of a package deal right now."

"Is that right?" I chuckle.

"Yup."

"I'll take you however I can get you, so Bradley it is," I say with a smile.

"Mia and I used to have a major crush on him in high school —not that we still don't now."

"Alright, alright. Are you trying to make me jealous?"

"Maybe?" She laughs, squeezing me tighter.

I smile at her. "Breakfast?"

"I have to tutor soon, but I probably have time for a quick egg sandwich. I'll make some for us after I shower." She untangles herself from me but not without a groan in protest from me first. She swats my hand away but crawls back on the mattress, giving me a quick kiss on the forehead.

"I'll be right out." She smiles and saunters out of the room toward the bathroom. My gaze follows her, thinking how damn lucky I am that she actually wants to be with me, too. She came into my life like a freaking tidal wave, my feelings for her only getting stronger every single minute that she's been here. I'm shamelessly all in with her, and I'm gonna do my damn best every single day to not screw this up.

I pull on some sweatpants and head for the kitchen to make some coffee. I slide a mug to Paige when she joins me, and she takes a quick sip before pulling a frying pan out of the drawer.

I take the carton of eggs out of the fridge while she grabs a spatula from the drawer. I toast some English muffins and prep the cheese slices while she flips the eggs.

A faint knock on the door has both of us looking over in

surprise. My family never knocks, so it's not any of them, and we aren't expecting anybody else as far as I know. I wonder who it is.

"I'll get it," I say, running my hand briefly down her back.

I pull the door open, and my eyes lock with my ex—Alicia— the girl I dated before Sabrina. My stomach twists in a knot.

What is she doing here?

"Alicia?"

She looks nervous, tucking a strand of blonde hair behind her ear. "Hi, Matt."

"Uh...come on in." I hold the door open for her and gesture at the kitchen. "This is Paige. My girlfriend."

Alicia's stride falters, hesitation obvious on her already anxious face. Her eyes lock on Paige, and then they drift back to me.

"Maybe I should come back another time," she says.

"Alicia." I stop her before she can retreat back into the hall. I need to know why she's here. And why she looks nervous. "Come in. Is something wrong?"

She blows out a steadying breath and takes a seat at the table, bringing her hands out in front of her. Her fingers pick at her nails nervously.

"Everything alright?" I ask again, sliding into the chair across from her, curiosity getting the best of me. It's been a few months since I've seen her, and we broke up on good terms. We were both in agreement that we weren't right for each other—

"I'm pregnant," she blurts out, interrupting my thoughts. The clink of a spatula dropping behind me does little to distract me from the pit that immediately forms in my stomach and the wave of nerves that rush over my skin.

"You're what?" I choke out.

"I'm sorry. I knew if I didn't just blurt it out, I wouldn't have the courage to say it."

My brain starts running a thousand miles a minute, re-tracing the end of our relationship, any hints she would have given me, why she would be here.

"It's yours," she confirms softly, looking down at her hands in her lap.

I'm frozen, unsure what to do. The tightness in my chest gives way to shock, my heart feeling like it might pound right out of my body. I finally manage to clear my throat.

"How is that possible?"

"I'm about three months along. I found out shortly after we broke up, and I've been trying to work up the nerve to tell you ever since. I should have told you sooner. I'm sorry," she whispers, glancing behind me at Paige.

Paige.

Alicia.

Baby.

Mine.

"Fuck." I run my hands down my face. I'm going to be a dad? How does somebody process this kind of news—before even having breakfast, no less?

"Listen, I don't want to step on any toes here. I obviously respect the fact that you're in a relationship. I'm not trying to get back together or anything. We'll just have to figure out a way to co-parent as best we can—"

"I'm sorry." I stand up, cutting through the jumbled fog of thoughts in my head. I can't take another word right now. I need to be alone to make sense of what this means.

"I need some air."

I rush out the front door, slamming the door behind me, ignoring the little voice in my head that's telling me to check on Paige.

26

PAIGE

I put one foot in front of the other on the way to school, mentally coaxing my legs to not be as numb as the rest of me right now. To say I'm shocked would be an understatement. Matt's going to have a baby. He's gonna be a dad. With another woman. What does that mean for us? Are we going to stay together?

Shit, am I ready for that? I love kids, but am I ready to be in a relationship with someone who's going to have one of his own? Am I ready for whatever step-mom role I would be fulfilling?

My heart sinks, remembering how perfect last night was, how incredibly happy I was waking up next to him. When his arms were wrapped comfortably around me, I was imagining how amazing it would be to build a life with him somehow. My feelings for him far overshadow the small fact that we live in different places. We would be stupid not to pursue something just because we don't live in the same state. That would get worked out eventually. The life we could have together would be worth it.

That was all completely shattered when Alicia showed up. Who knows what's going to happen now? I really do like Matt, more than I ever expected to, but is our relationship too new to weather something as big as this?

I thought about calling him on my way over here to check on him, but I ultimately decided it would be best to give him some space to process everything. I don't want to crowd him. I'll see him later on at the apartment and see where his head's at.

After Matt stormed out of the apartment, I tried my best to politely comfort Alicia, who had started crying. My heart aches for her, too. I can only imagine how scared she must be, and it must have taken a lot of courage for her to finally tell him. She seems like a genuinely nice person, and I didn't get any threatening vibes from her at all.

After helping her calm down and feeding her Matt's egg sandwich, I gently ushered her out and rushed to get ready for tutoring. Nothing will make me late again for Elliot, not even a bomb like this.

The rest of the walk to school passes by in a blur. Trying my best to ignore the lingering nerves and clear my head, I push open the door and head to the library. After a few minutes of mindlessly pulling books and gathering worksheets, I hear, "Hey, Miss C.!"

Ruby comes skipping into the library, followed closely by Graham. I expect Elliot to saunter in last like he usually does, but instead, Principal Murphy simply waves and retreats back down the hall quickly.

"Hi, Ruby. Hi, Graham. No Elliot today?" I ask as they slide into their chairs with their pencil pouches.

Graham shrugs. "No clue. He wasn't at the office."

The pit that was already growing in my stomach gets heavier.

I hope he's alright. He's never missed a session before. In fact, he's usually dropped off early.

I know he's been starting to find comfort being here, so it doesn't sit well with me that he's missing a day. I add that worry to the list of things I try to force to the back of my mind as I pass out some worksheets.

"Alright, let's get to work, guys," I say, doing my best to keep my voice steady and focus on the task at hand, hoping that Elliot will eventually walk through that door.

"Can we do our work outside today, Miss C.?" Ruby asks, flipping one of her pigtails with her finger.

"You know what, I like that idea, Ruby. Some fresh air sounds great." We gather our things and walk out the back door, past the playground, to our favorite spot under the palm tree. As usual, the heat from the sun glares down on us, so the three of us squeeze into the circle of shade on the grass.

"Can I read first?" Ruby asks, filtering through the stack of books I picked out.

"No fair! You always read first," Graham whines.

"It's okay, guys. We have plenty of time to read. In fact, you can both read twice today if you'd like."

They've both come so far in their reading comprehension this summer. I'd say they're pretty much up to grade level. I'm confident they'll have no problem keeping up with their peers in the fall.

Elliot, on the other hand, still has a ways to go when it comes to feeling confident participating in the classroom. We only have a few tutoring sessions left, so I hope whatever kept him from coming today doesn't happen again.

We spend the next couple hours reading books, going through phonics worksheets, and practicing some addition with math cubes.

The time passes quickly, constant worry for both Elliot and

Matt consuming the back of my mind, never completely going away despite how much I try.

When the clock strikes the top of the hour, we gather our stuff and head back to the front office. I wait with them in the hallway until their parents arrive to pick them up.

"Bye, Miss C.!" Ruby gives me a hug before racing outside to meet her mom.

"See ya later," Graham says once his dad's car pulls up outside.

"Bye, Graham. See you next time!" I force my voice to sound chipper, and then I immediately walk past the front desk and knock gently on Principal Murphy's office door.

"Come on in!" she calls, sounding distracted.

I ease the door open, forcing a smile when she looks up from the pile of paperwork on her desk.

"Hey, I just wanted to check on Elliot. Do you know why he was gone today? It's not like him to miss a day."

The look on her face sends a surge of panic down to my stomach. Stress, disappointment, and exhaustion all flash across her face at the same time as she inhales a big breath. The panic settles in my stomach and doesn't dissipate. This can't be good.

"His caseworker called me this morning. Apparently, his foster parent is choosing to terminate her contract. Says she doesn't want to be in charge of Elliot anymore." She presses her fingers to the bridge of her nose.

Anger and disbelief rush down my spine. "She can do that?"

"I guess." She sighs, shaking her head.

"So what happens now?"

She blows out another breath. "He's with his caseworker now at her office. She's trying to figure out a new foster family option for him."

The image of Elliot being shuffled around like a pawn in a chess game flashes across my mind, and it makes me feel overwhelmingly nauseated.

"So, he's gonna be moved to a new home?"

"That's the goal—depending on how long it takes to find a new one. There's a huge shortage of foster families here on Oahu. Depending on where he'll be, he might not be coming back to this school." She looks weary and defeated, matching my own emotions.

I feel like I'm gonna be sick. Poor Elliot. He must be terrified, not knowing what's going to happen or where he'll go. My heart aches for him, and anger-fueled determination rushes through me. There must be some way I can help. I'm one of the few people in this world willing to advocate for this boy, and like hell if I'm going to abandon him when he needs someone the most.

The overpowering need to protect him overshadows any other thoughts, and I suddenly know exactly what I want to do.

What I need to do.

After getting his caseworker's phone number, I rush out the school doors and down the stairs. I find a bench along the sidewalk to sit on, pulling my phone out to shoot Matt a quick text first.

27

MATT

Paige: Call me when you're ready to talk.

I study the text that Paige sent me two days ago, just like I have every hour since I first read it. Guilt rushes through me that I didn't call her right away. I should have called her before she even sent that text, but I'm just not ready to hear what she has to say yet.

My entire world has turned upside down, and my life will never be the same. Being responsible for another human is absolutely terrifying, and I'm having a hard time dialing down the panic that keeps creeping up.

I don't know what she's thinking, and I'm not ready to hear it if she says she wants out. I can't handle that on top of everything else yet.

Not that I would blame her. She's been wanting to take things slow and casual, and this is definitely the opposite of that. I wouldn't fault her if she didn't want to deal with my baggage anymore.

Baggage isn't the right word. That feels wrong. My child, as unexpected and surreal as this feels right now, is not and will never be a burden. That much, I know. It's pretty much all I know.

Everything is up in the air right now. What the hell am I going to do about Alicia? How are we going to make co-parenting work? How am I going to take care of a baby? Can I provide for it with my bartending job? And where does Paige fit into it all?

After I left the apartment the other day, I somehow ended up at the beach, although I don't remember walking there. I watched some surfers ride waves, then paddle back out to catch another wave repeatedly while I let my mind go numb. I sat there for a long time, lost in a haze of anxiety and fear until I finally wound up at my parents' house.

My mom must have called an emergency family meeting because shortly after I told my mom and dad everything, my sisters all showed up. I'm not sure if their constant attention and chatter helped at all, but at least it felt familiar—like home. John even showed up at some point to just sit next to me. I'm assuming he heard from Paige.

My mom's been making my favorite meals, making sure I'm eating. It's been the only thing that's taken some of the sting of reality away, and I guess I haven't been ready to go back to my real life yet. I'm not trying to avoid my responsibilities. I'm just trying to approach this in the best possible way. Giving myself time to think things through before I react seems like the right thing to do.

"How are you feeling?" my mom asks gently, setting a plate of pancakes next to a glass of orange juice, then leaning over the kitchen counter toward me. Uneasiness tinged with nausea spreads down my chest, pooling in my stomach at the thought of trying to put my feelings into words. I don't really know how to explain what I'm feeling right now.

"A little lost, I guess," I say, forcing a bite of pancake down my throat. "Not sure if I can handle being a dad," I admit. She's always had this sneaky way of getting me to open up and spill my feelings to her, especially if she's feeding me at the same time. She connects with people she loves by making food and sharing it with them. It's one of the things that makes her such an amazing mom. I'll be lucky if I'm half the parent she is.

"Matthew," she says softly. "First, you can do anything you set your mind to. You know that. That's how we raised you. Second, I'm not going to lie to you and say that this is an ideal situation or even that it won't be hard, because it most definitely will be. Being a dad will be the most important job you're ever going to do. It'll also be the most rewarding. I promise you, when you eventually hold that precious gift in your arms, you'll be willing to move heaven and earth for them. That's where your strength will come from. Everything else, you'll figure out. It'll fall into place. You have the strength to handle this, Matt. I know you do."

The sting of tears behind my eyes threatens to overflow, but I do my best to blink them away. I clear my throat and manage a shaky smile.

"Have you talked to Alicia or Paige yet?"

"Not yet," I clear my throat again. "I'll call Alicia after I eat. Then, it's probably time to head back to the apartment. I'll talk to Paige there."

She studies me and nods her head. When I push off the chair, she comes around and wraps me in a hug. She pulls back slightly, cupping my face with her hands.

"You, Matthew Swanson, are going to make an amazing father," she whispers with such conviction that if she tells me enough times, I might just believe her.

"Thanks, Ma." I kiss her cheek and retreat up the stairs to my childhood bedroom. Walking into it has me feeling like I'm thirteen again, when the biggest problem in my life was whose house to play at after school. Pictures of Kelly Slater and other surfing posters fill the walls, and my mom still has the same blue-and-red-checkered comforter on the queen bed.

I have a seat on the corner of the bed, the mattress dipping with my weight, and I inhale a deep breath. I pull up Alicia's contact info in my phone and press the green call button before I can talk myself out of it.

"Hello?" she answers anxiously after the first ring, like she's been waiting for me to call. I suddenly feel terrible that I haven't made an effort to contact her before now. In this moment, I promise myself to put her and the baby's needs before my own from here on out.

"Hey… I'm sorry I haven't called."

"It's okay," she says weakly. A few seconds pass, both of us trying to find the right words to say.

"So, you're pregnant, huh?" She snorts at the genius words that fly out of my mouth.

"Yes…I am. I'm sorry again for not telling you sooner." The regret is obvious in her voice.

"I wish you would have. Then you wouldn't have been living with it alone the last few months. I could have been there for you."

"What would you have done, Matt?" she asks. "We wouldn't have gotten back together. I didn't want that."

"No. I wouldn't have wanted that either. But I would have made sure you were alright. That's my job now. Have you been feeling good?"

"The first ten weeks were pretty rough. I threw up almost every day."

"Ish. Sorry to hear that."

"I'm feeling much better now. I have an ultrasound next

month if you want to come with. We could find out the gender then—if you want to find out," she says.

"I'd love to." After a brief moment of silence, I continue. "I'm here to support you in any way you need, okay? Just because we aren't together doesn't mean I won't be there. Anything at all, okay? That's my baby in there, and I want to make sure you're both taken care of."

"Thanks, Matt," she says with genuine appreciation and relief. After making a plan to talk soon to figure out the big details, I hang up the phone feeling like a weight's been lifted off my shoulders. I'm confident in the fact that Alicia and I are not meant to be together, but I am determined to do my absolute best to support her in any way that I can.

By no means would I say that I'm over the shock of everything, but at least Alicia and I are on the same page. That helps.

Now it's time to see where Paige is at.

After saying goodbye to my mom, I head back to the apartment. The whole walk there, I try to come up with a list of my greatest attributes. Not to convince Paige to still be with me, but just to have on hand to confirm that she'd be making the right choice if she did. I'm putting the ball entirely in her court on this one. As much as I desperately want to, I won't beg her to be with me. That wouldn't be fair. I'm more than willing to walk this road with her by my side, but only if she's all in, too.

Arriving at my front door brings a flood of new nerves to the surface of my skin. I brace myself to be prepared and accepting of any choice Paige makes, no matter how much it crushes me. I blow a deep breath out and push the front door open. I'm met with silence—no sign of Paige.

Maybe she's tutoring.

Or with Mia.

"Paige?" I call out.

No answer. I throw my keys on the table and head down the

hallway. The door to her room is open, and I catch a glimpse of her bare nightstand.

No. No. No.

I walk far enough in the doorway to see that all of Paige's belongings are gone.

Everything.

Gone.

I collapse onto the corner of the bed, completely gutted. My head falls into my hands, and I work my fingers over my forehead, attempting to distract myself from the pain in my chest.

I can't blame her for leaving, but damn, does it tear me to shreds. I've literally lived and breathed for Paige since the moment she came here, and she was finally mine. It's absolutely devastating that it was only for one night.

I let the pain wash over me, trying to accept the choice she made. But the only thing I'm confident in is that it's going to take a hell of a long time to get over her.

28

PAIGE

"Matt!" I call as soon as I see him coming out of his apartment. Shock completely takes over his face, and he turns cautiously toward me. An audible sigh of relief escapes my mouth. It feels so good to see him, and it's taking everything in me to not run into his arms right now. I slowly, carefully, walk the rest of the way until I'm standing just an arm's length from him.

"What are you doing here?" His eyes lock with mine, the intensity behind them not clearly conveying what he's thinking.

"I came to talk to you," I say simply. "You never called."

"I came back yesterday and saw that you moved out. I guess I assumed you made up your mind and didn't want to hear from me," he says with obvious pain in his voice that matches the pain in my chest. It's been such an emotional whirlwind the last several days, and I can't help the tears as they come to the surface and start spilling over.

This thing always happens with my mom, where I can't help

the emotions that spill over as soon as I see her. I can hold it all in and keep myself put together all day long and through most circumstances, but the second I see my mom, the tears can't be stopped. The same thing is happening now with Matt.

Looking into his eyes seems to make every single pillar of armor that I've built and have been leaning on the last few days get weaker and weaker until I feel completely exposed, the tears falling uncontrollably now.

"Hey," he whispers softly, "come here." He wraps me in his arms, and even though I can't seem to control the crying, I also feel like I can take a deep breath for the first time in days. I bring my arms around his waist, and we stand just like that, in the middle of the hallway, holding each other.

I get lost in the comfort of him, breathing in his crisp cedar scent with every deep breath until the tears eventually stop. He runs his hands slowly down my back.

"Do you want to come in and talk?" he whispers gruffly.

My tear-stained cheek nods against his T-shirt.

He grabs my hand and leads me inside while I wipe at the mascara under my eyes. He pulls back a chair at the table, and as soon as he's sitting, he pulls me sideways onto his lap with no hesitation from me, like we both want to be as close as possible. Even with all the unknowns on the state of our relationship, I can't help but want to be touching him.

"You okay?" His brows furrow with worry, eyes roaming all over me.

I sigh, giving a slight nod. "Yeah…sorry about that."

"No. Don't do that. Don't apologize for being upset. Listen, I don't blame you for leaving. As much as it kills me, I get why you don't want to be with me—"

"Matt," I cut him off. "I've been giving you space to process everything. That's why I didn't call you, but I didn't move out because of you. It's just…a lot has happened since you left that morning."

"Like what?" His grip on my hip tightens, bracing himself for whatever I have to say.

"You know one of the students I was tutoring, the one who was in foster care—Elliot? Well, his foster mom decided to terminate her contract early. He didn't show up when I went to tutor that day. He was with his caseworker, waiting to be transferred to a different home, and I just couldn't let him be shuffled around again to people who might not care about him or have enough resources to give him the attention he deserves. And I just couldn't sit back and let it happen. I just couldn't, Matt." Tears sting my eyes once again.

"Shh…it's okay." He runs his hand up the side of my waist to my back, soothing the tension away with every stroke.

"So, I offered to be his foster parent," I blurt out.

"You what?" he asks in surprise.

"I offered to be his foster parent. Well, technically, I applied for an emergency foster-parent license so I could take him. I filled out the forms and did all the required background checks and everything. Normally, things like that take a while, but she was able to pull some strings and push it through right away." His hand gently squeezes the top of my shoulder, a subtle sign that he's listening.

"I had to show proof of employment and proof of residence. I couldn't be living with a roommate, so that's why I had to move out. Luckily, Pat, the landlord, had a vacancy at the end of the hall on this same floor, so I signed a lease for that one. Mia and John came over to help me move before Elliot arrived yesterday. Mia threatened to call off the engagement if John told you." A small laugh bubbles out. "I didn't want to add more to your plate. You're going through enough as it is. I wanted you to process all of that without worrying about me."

"Wow," he breathes out, bringing his chin to rest on the top of my shoulder. "That's a lot, Paige."

It is a lot. But at the same time, it was one of the easiest decisions I've ever made. I've always said I wouldn't move to another state for a guy I've only known for a short amount of time, but I would absolutely, one-thousand percent, move for Elliot. Without question.

"Wait, did you say proof of employment?" he asks, bringing his head upright to look me in the eyes.

"I did. I accepted a permanent teaching position at Honu Elementary. Principal Murphy was completely on board when I told her my plan, and she was happy to offer me a position teaching third grade in the fall."

"So, you're here to stay?" His eyes glimmer with cautious hope.

"I'm here as long as Elliot needs me. I don't know how long that will be, but I'm not giving up on him."

He smiles and squeezes me tighter. "I'm proud of you."

I return the smile and get lost for a moment in his eyes, slipping into and savoring the connection I missed out on the last few days.

"How are you doing?" I ask, suddenly nervous for his answer. "I've been so worried about you."

He heaves a sigh, blowing out a steadying breath. "Things are still really fresh and raw. A part of me still doesn't believe that I'm gonna be a dad. But I'm starting to come to terms with it. I mean, I can't change the situation, so I might as well make the most of it. Try and be the best dad I can possibly be."

I bring my arms around his neck and say quietly, "You're going to be an amazing dad, Matt. Your child is lucky to have you." And I mean it. Whether I'll end up being a part of his life or not, I know for certain that his child is already so fortunate. He'll be the most fun, playful, easygoing, and loyal dad ever.

He responds with a smile, bringing his eyes to mine.

"Should we talk about us?" his voice cracks.

"Matt…" I trail off, not knowing what to say.

"'Cause I'm not getting back together with Alicia. That was

never even a thought that crossed my mind." His eyes are still locked on mine. "I still only want to be with you. But I understand that I'm a package deal now, and maybe it's not what you want to sign up for right now. Shit, things are complicated right now for both of us. It's your call, but I'm still all in if you are. I just want you to know that before you say anything else."

Butterflies flutter in my stomach, and warmth spreads through my chest. What I wouldn't give to stay curled up with him forever and forget both of our messy, complicated lives.

"Matt, I would love to be all in right now, too...but I don't know how much of myself I can give. I need to be fully there for Elliot right now. He's my top priority," I say. "But that's not me closing the door on us. There would be a lot to figure out together, and I don't know exactly how we fit into each other's lives now...but I guess I'm not ruling it out?"

"I'll take however much of you I can get," he says softly, bringing his lips to mine. I lean into his kiss, letting my heart rate get gradually faster. "We can take it day by day," he says between kisses. His hands grip at my hips, pulling me even closer against him. Eventually, I break away, bringing my hands to the sides of his neck and resting my forehead against his.

"Okay," I whisper. He nods slowly with his eyes still closed, arms still firmly wrapped around me.

"I should be heading back," I say. "Mia offered to stay with Elliot in my apartment while I came to talk to you. I don't want to be gone for too long."

"Okay." He loosens his grip so I can climb off his lap, but he grabs my hand before I can get too far. His eyes lock with mine, and he slowly rises to stand without looking away. He pulls me close, resting his arms loosely on my lower back. I place my hands on the solid muscle of his chest.

"I'm here for you, in any way you'll let me be, okay? I'm just right down the hall. Let me know if you need anything."

"I will." I smile up at him, press my lips to his to kiss once, and then wrap my arms around his torso to squeeze him in a hug. We stay like that until I can feel his heartbeat match mine, our hearts syncing together in the most comforting of ways.

"I'll call you later," I say, releasing myself from him, giving him one last squeeze with my hand, and heading for the door. Before I shut the door behind me, I glance back one more time to find Matt exactly where I left him, eyes still locked on me.

29

PAIGE

"Do you like making sandcastles?" I ask Elliot, handing him a shovel.

He shrugs, sliding his glasses up the bridge of his nose. "I don't come to the beach a lot," he says quietly. My heart tugs, wondering what kid growing up in Hawaii doesn't have a lifetime of digging in the sand by his age? I know the answer—one who was forgotten about, cast aside, let down by the system.

This sweet boy has been dealt a crummy hand in life so far, but I plan to do whatever I can to turn that around for him. Whether I stay here forever or just stay until he gets adopted by a decent family, it doesn't matter to me. No matter how long it takes, I'll be here for him any way I can, even if it means putting my old life in Minnesota on hold.

My parents were pretty shocked when I told them what I was planning to do. They couldn't understand why I would make such a big decision after such a short amount of time, but once I explained how strongly I feel about helping Elliot, they seemed to come around a little bit. I'm sure it'll take some time for them to fully be on board, but that's okay. They don't know Elliot, and they don't know how special he is.

The bond we were starting to form during our tutoring sessions has only gotten stronger since Thursday when we were erratically thrown together, both of us finding ourselves in a new apartment with a new person to all of a sudden share a space with. Both of our lives were forever changed that day.

As soon as Elliot was dropped off at my new apartment, I showed him the room that I set up for him. Mia and I had run to Target while we waited for my background check to clear, and we picked up all things dragons. He has a red dragon comforter on his bed and a few dragon posters for the wall. We even picked up a small desk for the corner of his room and stocked it with some fresh art supplies for him.

He seemed pretty emotionally exhausted when he first arrived, but he did show a faint smile or two when exploring his new room. Being responsible for the way his eyes became slightly less clouded when he ran his hand along the desk was enough to fuel my determination and commitment to him.

He didn't know what time he normally went to bed at night, so I opted for an early bedtime in hopes of us both getting a good night of sleep. After he climbed into bed, I could tell his nerves were heightened, and tears were starting to rim his eyes. I asked him if he wanted me to stay for a little while, if me being in the room might help.

"Yes, please," he had replied with a shaky voice.

I spent at least an hour sitting on his desk chair, watching him fall asleep, thinking about this huge responsibility I just signed up for, and hoping like hell that I'll know what to do and be enough for him.

I didn't hear him make any noise throughout the night from my room, but when I came out the next morning, I found him just standing near the living room, feet lightly shuffling back and forth, unsure of what to do.

I did my best to plaster a bright smile on my face and invited him into the kitchen to make unicorn toast for breakfast. He looked at me like I had grown another head while sleeping, and it made both of us break into much-needed laughter.

We worked quietly but comfortably as we mixed food coloring into cream cheese and spread it across a few pieces of toast. We topped them with blueberries and sprinkles before touching them together in a cheers and devouring them.

We spent the rest of that day and the next two days just being with each other. We played board games, watched movies, and did quite a bit of coloring. I ordered a bean-bag chair for the corner of his room so I have a comfy place to sit at bedtime since he seems to want me there when he falls asleep.

He still doesn't make a lot of eye contact, and we definitely have a ways to go as far as him being completely comfortable, but I'm okay with that. I'm just trying to be consistently there for him, show him that I'm not going anywhere, and hopefully, he'll eventually trust me. I'm in it for the long haul.

"When we went on vacations to a beach when I was a kid, I used to always bury my brother, Caleb, in the sand up to his chest," I tell him, running my fingers through the sand. "Then, I'd sculpt the sand around him to make it look like he was a mermaid. I bet we could totally convince Matt to let us do that to him, too."

Half of his mouth curves up into a smile.

We haven't left the apartment much at all, and besides meeting Mia when she came to hang out with him so I could talk to Matt the other day, he hasn't really met anyone else. When we made plans to come to the beach today, I figured it might be a good time to see if Matt would like to meet us here. I asked Elliot if he'd like to meet another one of my friends, and as soon as he agreed, I wasted no time texting Matt. I haven't seen him since I left his apartment that day, and I miss him so much it hurts.

I had gotten so used to sharing every little part of my day with him, and I've definitely felt a loss from being apart from him. I can't really let my mind look to the future and picture what a life with him would look like, given both of our circumstances. All I know is that, right now, I miss him like hell.

As if summoned by my thoughts, Matt calls out from behind us.

"Did anyone order some shaved ice?"

Elliot looks up, and I turn around to find him holding two cups wrapped in napkins, spoons sticking out the sides, colorful ice rapidly melting down his fingers. He has a seat next to me, handing me the red one with little bits of strawberries on top.

"Sorry, it kinda melted on the walk over here," he says apologetically.

"It's okay." I grin at him, feeling a surge of butterflies in my stomach when my eyes roam down his bare chest. "Matt, this is Elliot. Elliot, this is my friend, Matt."

"Hey, buddy," Matt says. "I didn't know what your favorite flavor was, so I got you rainbow flavor. Is that alright?"

Elliot eyes him cautiously, then slowly nods, taking the cup in silence. He scoops a bite into his mouth, keeping his focus down at the sand.

"How are you?" he asks me.

I respond with a smile. "Elliot and I are trying to make a sandcastle."

After holding my eyes for a split second, Matt crawls away from me to sit on the other side of Elliot. He sifts through the bag of sand toys and pulls out a mini rake.

"Do you mind if I dig a moat around your sand castle?"

Elliot keeps his head down but gives him a small shrug of approval. I watch as Matt starts digging into the sand, Elliot scooping ice into his mouth with one hand, shoveling sand into a bucket with the other. I sit in silence, my heart jumping, watching them together.

At one point, I catch Matt stealing glances at Elliot, stopping to stare for brief seconds at a time. I wonder what's going through his mind—if he's thinking about becoming a father, having a kid of his own.

Eventually, I join them, using the corner of a shovel to carve small windows into the lopsided pillars of our masterpiece. Matt and I make easy conversation while Elliot plays.

"What's your favorite color, Elliot?" Matt asks casually, pouring ocean water into the moat he built.

I try to not show the surprise on my face when he answers with a quiet, "Red."

"Right on. Mine's blue. Paige?" Matt lifts his eyebrows up, eyes shifting to my direction. A stray strand of dirty-blond hair falls over his forehead, and my breath gets caught in my throat.

"Black," I say simply.

"Black?" he asks incredulously. "Who has black as their favorite color?" he teases. I can't help but smile when I catch a glimpse of Elliot starting to smile.

"What are you, a witch?" Matt lifts the corner of his mouth into a cocky smirk.

"Hey, now," I laugh, tossing my shovel gently at him.

"Okay. What's your favorite animal?" He directs his attention back to Elliot.

"Dolphin," he says in just a slightly higher volume.

"Sea turtle for me. Paige?"

"Definitely dog." I frown, thinking about Harley back at home. Besides my parents, he's the one thing I'll miss the most about home, and it hurts knowing I won't be seeing him for a while.

"Favorite food?" Matt tosses his shovel back in the bag.

After several seconds of Elliot not saying anything, I chime in.

"That's a toss-up for me between tacos and unicorn toast." I'm proud of myself for getting through that with a straight face.

Elliot pushes his lips together, trying his best to hold it all in.

"Unicorn toast? What in the world is that?" Matt demands, his eyes imploring mine.

Laughter bursts out of me, and Elliot follows shortly after. We're lost in a fit of hysterics, me falling over to my side onto the sand, Elliot hunching forward, covering his face with his hand. Matt can't help but join in, probably laughing just at the sight of us.

I eventually shift flat on my back, spreading my arms out on the sand, catching my breath. As I gaze up at the sun, my heart swells at the lingering sound of Elliot laughing. I've never heard him laugh before, and I have to blink back tears to stop them from falling.

It's not lost on me how significant this moment is. I wonder how many times, if any, Elliot's felt carefree and happy enough to laugh like he is right now. I wish like hell that number would be a lot, but I just don't think that's the case.

After a few deep breaths to calm myself, I sit back up. I smile and wink at Elliot, who smiles back at me.

"I have no idea what just happened," Matt says. "But you're still up, little man. Favorite food?"

Elliot answers quickly this time. "Spaghetti."

"Oh, good choice. Hey, I make a killer spaghetti and meatball dinner. Maybe you two should swing by one night, and I can make it for you?"

I wait to see how Elliot will respond. When his face lights up and he nods, I smile at Matt.

"That sounds nice," I say, resisting the urge to grab for his hand.

"Well, what do you think, Elliot? Should we pack up and head back?"

"Sure."

"Wait, let me take a picture of our amazing sandcastle first," Matt says. "For documentation."

He snaps a quick picture, and the three of us start gathering the shovels, buckets, and towels we brought. Elliot falls into step next to me, Matt on the other side, as we walk off the beach. As we walk, Matt mutters in my ear, "You still have to explain what unicorn toast is."

30

MATT

"Now, here's the ultimate question, Elliot. Meatballs or no meatballs?" I offer a spoon with spaghetti sauce on the tip to him. He takes it and tastes it with the tip of his tongue very carefully.

His face remains completely neutral, which makes Paige snort a laugh from the kitchen table.

"You gonna give me something? Anything? Is it good?" I probe.

Elliot gives the slightest nod of approval.

"I'll take it. I'm qualifying that as the official Elliot stamp of approval. And I'm gonna pretend you said yes to meatballs since they're almost done," I say.

He shuffles back to the seat next to Paige. She was right. There is something special about this kid. This is only the second time I've been around him, but he's definitely growing on me.

How could you not like him? He's sweet in a cautious, timid way that makes it almost impossible not to feel for the kid.

I'm so glad Paige said yes when I invited them over for spaghetti tonight. Being around her and Elliot has been the only thing that's helped to take my mind off the persistent nausea that's been settling on the surface of my skin. I haven't been able to shake the nerves, no matter how hard I try.

I met up with Alicia yesterday at a local coffee shop, and we went through our calendars for the next few months. I don't want to miss a single doctor's appointment or baby-related thing. We also figured out a schedule for when the baby's born. The baby will stay with Alicia for the majority of the time right away, with me having frequent visits—at least for the first couple weeks. Then, we'll slowly work our way up to some sort of 2-2-3 day schedule. I'll have to figure out a way to work my bartending hours around a baby. I can't exactly be staying out till bar close with a newborn baby at home.

Even though I feel slightly better after our talk, after figuring out some sort of a plan, it also did nothing to ease my nerves. Actually, I think it only heightened them. In the span of a few months, I'll have a child. And eventually, I'll be responsible for taking care of that child all by myself. I can barely take care of myself. Will my bartending hours and lifestyle be conducive to baby life?

Being with Elliot tonight seems to be softening the blow a little bit. It's a no-pressure way to get some kid practice in. I think spending time with him and Lily will help get me into dad mode—if Paige is alright with that, of course.

She comes up next to me to grab some plates from the cabinet, then slides the drawer out for some utensils. It feels nice, her being so comfortable at my place, moving around seamlessly like she used to. I've missed it.

"Alright, Elliot, you want to come grab a plate?" Paige asks.

I pile some noodles on Elliot's plate, followed by Paige's, and top both with sauce and a couple meatballs. I throw a piece of garlic bread on each of their plates.

I make a plate of my own and join them at the table, taking a seat in the chair directly across from Paige.

"Wow, this looks good," she says, admiring her plate of food. I take the first bite, allowing my eyes to roam over her. Her dark hair's pulled back in a braid that's falling over one shoulder. She's wearing the hell out of a cream-colored T-shirt and jean shorts.

"My dad's famous recipe," I say.

We eat in comfortable silence, both Paige and I exchanging a few glances after Elliot slurps up his spaghetti hungrily. He finishes way before we do and stands up.

"Bathroom?" he asks politely and quietly.

"Straight down that hall, the first door on the left."

As soon as he's out of sight, the visible shift in Paige's appearance makes my stomach drop. Her eyes all of a sudden look exhausted, and her shoulders slump slightly.

"Hey, you okay?" I ask. She gives me a weary smile, rubbing her fingers on her temples.

"I'm alright. Just stressed out, you know? Tired." She inhales a deep breath, and I can't help but move out of my chair to the one next to her.

Placing my arm around her shoulders, she curls toward me and places her head on my shoulder.

"I miss you," she whispers. My chest tightens because, dammit, I miss her, too. "I don't regret being Elliot's foster parent—at all. I know without a doubt that was the right thing to do." She shifts her head to look up at me. "I just miss being here sometimes—when it was just me and you. When the most stressful part of my day was dodging your flirting and swatting you away," she says with a small laugh.

I chuckle, feeling a sense of loss for our reality that wasn't so long ago, when all I worried about was feeling bored and unfulfilled at work. I rub my hand up and down her arm.

"Life kinda blew up in our faces, didn't it?"

She nods, bringing her arms around my torso in a firm grip. "Yeah, it did," she says softly, acknowledging the way our worlds completely turned upside down—at the same time, no less.

The bathroom door creaks open, and Paige unwraps her arms from me to settle back upright on her chair. I shift in my seat, glancing back toward Elliot.

"Anyone up for a walk to the beach to watch the sunset?" I say, mostly asking Elliot. He looks unsure and glances at Paige, like he's not used to being asked what he wants to do.

"It's up to you," she says, the bright smile back on her face. "We can go if you'd like, or if you're too tired, we can head back to the apartment. You choose. Either way is fine with me."

He thinks for a minute, then says, "Let's go."

"Right on," I say.

Paige clears our plates while I scoop the noodles and sauce into containers, then hand them to Elliot to place in the fridge. When dinner's all cleaned up, we head out to the beach.

We find the sidewalk, and Elliot finds his place walking right in between Paige and me. I can't help but wonder if this is my future. If Paige miraculously wants to be with me, this could maybe be us, except with my own child in between us.

"What are you up to this week?" Paige asks me.

I kick some sand to the side as I walk. "I have a shift at work tomorrow afternoon, and then I'm gonna swing by Marty's. He's been having some issues with his back, so I've just been showing up to help bartend when I have the time."

"He's actually letting you help?" She laughs.

"He didn't exactly ask me to, but he also doesn't kick me out when I slip behind the bar, so I'm thinking his back is worse than he lets on."

"Shoot. I hope he gets better soon."

"Me too. What about you? You two have any fun plans this week?"

"Nothing set in stone, probably a trip to the grocery store. Tutoring ended last week," Paige says with a smile, glancing down at Elliot. "Other than that, we'll see what we're up for, huh, Elliot?"

He nods in response. It feels good to chat mindlessly, talking about the mundane, everyday things we used to talk about. It feels familiar. Comfortable.

We stop to slip our shoes off once we hit the sand and walk until we find an empty spot right by the water. There's still a bit of daylight left, and I can't help but smile when Elliot starts digging his hands into the sand.

"Can I go in the water?" Elliot looks at Paige expectantly.

"Sure, but just until the water's up to your knees, okay?"

With a nod, he walks in, bending to run his hands over the top of the water. Paige scoots closer to me, bringing her arms out behind her, one threading between my arm that's resting on the sand. She lays her head on my shoulder, and her chest rises with a deep breath.

"You don't have to shoulder all of this yourself, Paige," I say quietly. "You can lean on me. I want to be there for you and Elliot." And I mean it. My feelings for Paige didn't just go away. Are they more complicated now? Absolutely. But they might be even stronger now after seeing the way she's handling this situation with Elliot. I'm willing to help him any way I can, too.

"I know," she says just as softly, staring at Elliot digging for seashells. "Thank you."

Elliot eventually joins us, and the sun slowly starts to set. We watch as the sky morphs into a colorful spread of yellow, orange, and pink. I've seen plenty of amazing sunsets growing up here, but this one somehow feels a little more special. Even though it's not particularly stunning, watching it with Paige and Elliot and seeing the way his face is lighting up makes it feel like the most significant sunset I've ever seen.

31

PAIGE

I push Matt's door open after knocking twice.

"Matt? I'm here," I say, walking through the door.

"Paige!" Tori exclaims, rushing over to me from the kitchen. "It's so good to see you! I was hoping you weren't gonna be scared off by my brother's irresponsible behavior." She wraps me in a hug, and I can't help but laugh.

"I'm still here...kind of," I say, not really knowing how to explain what Matt and I are right now.

"I heard about your situation with the foster kid. I just want you to know I think it's amazing what you're doing," she says sincerely.

"Thanks, Tori." I leave it at that, not feeling like going into details.

"Is Matt around? I asked if I could borrow some milk, and he told me to come right in."

"He's in the spare room with the rest of the sisters. They're helping him set it up for the baby. Go on back. He could probably use some saving," she laughs.

Mia's back at my apartment with Elliot. She came over to play board games with him while I make some cupcakes. I'm only short about ½ cup of milk, but luckily, Matt has some.

They were both completely engrossed in a game of Trouble when I left, so I guess ten extra minutes won't hurt.

I can hear Ava and Grace arguing over where to place the crib before I can even see inside the bedroom.

"Paige!" Emily smiles when she sees me. "Come on in! We could use another opinion."

The room is a complete disaster. The queen bed that was mine is gone, the floor now covered with baby supplies and bags of clothes scattered everywhere. The girls are rummaging through a tote of blankets while Matt is sitting on the floor next to a large box, crib assembly instructions in hand.

He looks up to me with complete exhaustion, his lips pushed together like if he opens his mouth, he'll regret what would spill out.

"Hi," I say, holding back a laugh. Tori comes in behind me, taking her place in an open space of floor next to an infant rocker.

"So, Grace and I think the crib should go along this wall," Emily says, gesturing toward the far wall. "And Ava thinks it should go here, along this wall."

"I'm telling you, it's the best option. That side shares a wall with the unit next door, and I guarantee you're not gonna want any possibility of extra noise when the baby's sleeping. This wall will be quieter. As the only one here with a child, I think my opinion should trump all of yours. What do you think, Paige?"

"Um, I guess I wouldn't want to put it by a shared wall, either. And you definitely don't want it by the window, so, yeah, I guess I agree with Ava. Sorry." I glance sheepishly at the other girls.

"Whatever!" Grace says to Ava. "Just because you're the only one who's had a baby, that doesn't mean that the rest of us haven't had years of experience, too. I seem to remember basically living at your house for the first couple months after Lily was born."

"Yeah! You didn't seem to mind our opinions then!" Emily retorts.

"Moving on," Tori says, "I scoured the internet and found two monitors that have the highest ratings. I bought both of them, and I'll just return the one we don't end up using."

"Good plan," Grace agrees.

Matt abruptly stands up, ushering me back into the hall. "Here, let me show you where the milk is."

"I think she knows where the milk is—"

He shuts the door behind him, cutting Tori off. "I'm about to lose it," he says, shaking his head. "They won't stop."

"They're clearly excited, huh?" I laugh.

"You could say that. After the initial shock of the baby news wore off, they all of a sudden started acting like this baby is theirs. I'm lucky if I can get a word in. I don't even know why I'm here."

"Did you expect anything different?" I ask with a smile. "You know they mean well."

His eyes search mine, and a slow smile spreads across his face. He opens his arms in invitation, saying a low, "Hi," as I step into his arms.

"Hi," I say back. We stand like that, wrapped in a hug for a few minutes, butterflies in my stomach going crazy. It feels so good to be completely engulfed by his strong body. I lift my head up and can't resist the urge to kiss him. He leans down and meets me halfway, our lips connecting in a brief kiss.

"How's Elliot?" he asks, releasing me but grabbing my hand as we walk to the kitchen.

"He's doing okay, I think. I can tell he's starting to get more comfortable with me. His caseworker stopped by this morning to check in, and she said she's shocked by how well he's doing. She's never seen him form an attachment to a foster parent like he has to me. So I guess I'm doing something right?"

He sets the carton of milk on the counter and pulls on my hand to bring me closer again. "That's amazing, Paige." He rests his free hand on my hip, the warmth of his hand burning through my clothes.

"I can't say I'm surprised, though. I see how you two are with each other. You're good for him."

I smile, letting his words send a wave of comfort through me. That's all I want. For Elliot to be happy.

"Thanks," I say. I close the rest of the space between us, resting my hand on his chest and tilting my head up. "I should get back."

He brings his head closer to mine, hovering just an inch from my lips. "Okay," he whispers, my eyes traveling from his mouth up to lock with his eyes.

"Don't mind me!" Emily bursts into the kitchen, skirting around us to grab her water bottle on the counter.

Matt sighs, resting his head on my forehead. I giggle, give him a quick kiss, and grab the milk.

"Thanks again for the milk. We'll bring it back later. Bye, Emily!"

Emily waves, and Matt's heated eyes follow me to the door. I throw him a wink that he loves so much and shut the door behind me.

Back at the apartment, Mia and Elliot are still hovering over the game, zeroed in on the board.

"Ahh, man! You're totally gonna beat me!" Mia cries as Elliot moves his last peg into his finish line, winning the game.

Elliot smiles at the board, proud of himself.

"That's the second time he's won," Mia says to me while putting the game pieces back in the box.

"Nice job, Elliot!" I laugh. "Wanna come help make the rest of these cupcakes?"

He slides off the couch and climbs up on a stool by the kitchen island. Mia follows him, and we all gather around the mixing bowls. I pour some milk into a measuring cup, then hand it to Elliot to pour into the bowl.

"How was Matt?" Mia asks me with a twinkle in her eye.

"Good," I answer. "His sisters were over, helping him get the spare room ready for the baby. He looked pretty overwhelmed." I laugh.

"I still can't believe he's gonna be a dad."

"Same," I say with a shake of my head.

We finish mixing the batter, then Mia helps Elliot scoop it into the cupcake pan.

"We should bring some to Matt when they're done," Elliot says quietly after I slip the pan into the oven.

"Great idea. I bet he'd love some," Mia says, ruffling the top of his head.

"I agree. We can bring some over and return the milk at the same time." I smile.

My heart swells, loving the fact that Elliot's not only starting to bond with me but also with the people who mean so much to me.

32

MATT

"Ready to see some dolphins, Elliot?" I securely fasten his life jacket and hoist him across the dock into the boat. Brian grabs him from inside, placing him on the bench seat. Paige grabs my hand and steps over the side, taking a seat next to Elliot. I hoist the cooler into the boat, then climb in myself.

I asked Elliot if he wanted to go on a dolphin-watching boat ride, and judging by his reaction, it's something he's never done before. His eyes almost completely bugged out of his head. He was stunned that I'd actually offered to take him.

"Why would you take me?" he had questioned, skeptical of my motives.

"Just for fun." I shrugged my shoulders. "Because I remembered that your favorite animal is a dolphin, and it was something I thought you'd enjoy. I like doing things for people I care about that I think will make them happy."

The smile that spread across his face, coupled with his eyes that darted between me and Paige, made my heart melt. This right here is exactly why I put thought into the things I do for other people. I like making them feel special and cared for. Elliot's reaction only solidified that, and I'm happy to do my part in showing him that people do care. That he means something to us. That he matters.

Tourists typically book an excursion on a catamaran to go dolphin sightseeing and then snorkeling, but that sounded like it might be a little too overwhelming and crowded for Elliot. Luckily, Brian didn't have any charters booked today, and he agreed to take us on his fishing boat up the west coast of Oahu— the best location for dolphin and whale sightings.

"Let's head out," Brian says, throwing the boat into reverse. I find a seat on the other side of Elliot, stretching my arm to rest behind their backs.

"My buddy, Brian, here is the best darn tour guide you could ask for," I tell Elliot.

"Thanks for bringing us, Brian. We really appreciate it," Paige tells him.

"Not a problem," Brian replies, pushing down on the throttle to move us through some waves. "At your service for the next two hours."

Normally, when we go out on Brian's boat, I take my role as co-captain very seriously, helping him as much as I can with the gear and offering helpful suggestions. But this time, I feel completely content right here next to Paige and Elliot. There's nowhere else I'd rather be than right next to both of them.

We boat along the shoreline, passing a few tourist catamarans that are filled with people. Along the way, Paige and I point out all the animals and sea life that we see. Off in the distance, a whale surfaces, blowing air out of its blowhole.

Elliot's mouth drops open as he pushes the prescription sunglasses Paige got for him farther up his nose.

"That's so cool," he says, his voice barely heard above the motor and the wind.

"There!" Paige shouts, pointing at two dolphins jumping out of the water on our left. Elliot squeals, covering his mouth with his hand.

"Pretty cool, huh?" I ask, patting him gently on the back. "I bet we'll see more."

We see several dolphins, Elliot gasping with each one he sees. At one point, I glance down and see Elliot's small hand resting on top of Paige's. Hers is palm down, flat against the seat between them. I catch Paige's eyes over the top of his head, and we exchange soft, knowing smiles. The significance of this moment isn't lost on either of us.

Eventually, Brian pulls back on the throttle, slowing to a stop.

"Turtle Canyon is right up ahead," he says, angling back toward us, pointing off to the right.

"Oh yeah, Turtle Canyon is a pretty cool spot," I tell them. "Green sea turtles hover above the reef while reef fish swim around them to clean their shells. There's usually a ton of them."

"I've got snorkel gear on board if you want to check it out?" Brian asks.

"Have you ever been snorkeling, Elliot?" I ask, already knowing the answer to that question but asking anyway.

He shakes his head. "Can we, please?" he asks hopefully.

Paige shoots me a glance, and we have another silent exchange. How can you say no to that?

"Sure, buddy," she says with a smile.

Brian brings us to a spot not far from another boat, and we help Elliot get situated with some goggles and a snorkel. Since he can't swim, we'll leave the life jacket on, and he can just dip his head below water. He should still be able to see plenty of turtles and fish that way.

I don't bother putting any gear on, wanting to focus on Elliot.

This is about him. Paige strips down to her dark-blue swimsuit, which I have a hard time not focusing on, and then puts on a mask and snorkel herself.

"Wait, before we do anything else, I absolutely need a picture of you in that gear," I laugh. She rolls her eyes but gives me a thumbs up for the picture. After taking one of her and Elliot together, the three of us swing our legs over the side of the boat and slide into the turquoise water.

Elliot grips my arm, getting used to floating in the water as gentle waves roll over us. He keeps a firm grip on me, and we just float like that for a few minutes until he seems to relax slightly.

"Alright, whenever you're ready, you can try dipping your head below the water and see what you can see," I say. "Remember to breathe through your mouth into the snorkel. If any water sneaks in your goggles, just let me know, and I'll tighten them."

He glances at Paige, who's treading water next to him, then he nods and very slowly lowers his face in, keeping a grip on my arm the whole time. The water's clear enough that I can see below us even from the surface. I spot at least six turtles hovering above the reef. There's a mix of surgeonfish, butterflyfish, and tang fish swarming around them.

Paige swims underwater a little ways to get a closer look. Elliot keeps his head under for a while, moving his head across the surface of the water. When Paige swims back up, Elliot lifts his head out of the water, too.

"I've never seen so many sea turtles!" Paige exclaims.

Elliot puts his head under a few more times until, eventually, he lifts his mask off.

"That's so cool," he says breathlessly as we make our way back to the boat that's drifted a little farther away. Brian helps pull Elliot and Paige in, and I hoist myself over.

I wrap a towel around my waist and hand a couple to Paige.

"What'd you think, Elliot?" she asks, wrapping him in a towel.

"I saw, like, ten turtles down there!" he exclaims, the volume of his voice breaching a normal level. I've never heard him talk this loud.

"Wasn't that awesome?" I ask, ruffling his hair. His eyes are gleaming as he looks up at me and nods.

"Now's probably a good time for a snack. Are you hungry?" Paige asks him.

"Sure," Elliot replies.

She digs through the cooler, pulling out a cheese tray she had put together earlier. She hands Elliot a juice box before grabbing three waters for the rest of us. We snack while watching for more dolphins in the distance, feeling the sun shining down on us. I can't help but be completely content and happy in this moment. I can't help but look forward to doing this exact thing with my own kid someday.

Before we know it, the cheese is gone, and we're completely dry. The humid air had quickly warmed us back up.

"Ready to head back?" Brian asks. We all agree and settle back into the bench seat behind him as he starts moving in the direction we came from.

The ride back is relaxed and comfortable. Elliot has one hand on Paige's knee, the other on mine, bracing himself with every wave we hit. As we near the marina, I help Brian get the lines ready and grab hold of the dock once we get close enough. We tie everything up and help Brian put everything else away.

After profusely thanking Brian, Paige and Elliot climb out of the boat. Elliot reaches for her hand again as they start walking off the dock.

"Thanks, brother." I shake Brian's hand and climb out myself, quickly catching up to them.

"That was fun today. Thanks for coming with me, guys," I tell them, tossing the Jeep keys in my hand.

"Thanks for taking us," Paige says sincerely, her emotion-filled eyes connecting with mine.

When we're just about to my car, Elliot says, mostly to himself, "I think that was the best day of my entire life."

Paige and I steal a glance at each other over his head. I can see the tears welling in her eyes, and damn if that doesn't make me start to get emotional, too. It feels good being able to provide such a special day for him. It feels like second nature. It feels more than right.

33

PAIGE

"You got it, Elliot! Keep pedaling! Just like we've been practicing," Matt shouts as he very carefully lets go of the back of the bike. He jogs behind him, staying close.

"Good job, E!" I call from the curb where I'm sitting. We found a quiet street near our apartment that we've been coming to every day for the past few days, either in the afternoon or after dinner, depending on Matt's work schedule. Elliot asked Matt to teach him how to ride a bike, and of course, he did not take that lightly. It's now Matt's top mission in life to teach him. Matt doesn't do anything halfway. When he commits to something, he's all in. It's one of the things I like most about him.

Elliot makes it a few feet on his own, and then the bike leans to the right. His foot catches his fall, avoiding completely falling onto the pavement.

"That was amazing, Elliot! You were doing that last part on

your own! Should we try again?" Matt asks as he helps steady the bike.

They get the bike straightened and ready for the next run as I watch with a smile on my face. Elliot and I have been gradually figuring out our new normal. Our new routine. I can tell he's starting to trust me more.

It's the way he's come out of his shell, the subtle hand grabbing, and the way he's wanting to try new things that tells me he is. I would do absolutely anything for that boy, and I'm pretty sure he knows it.

I let Elliot take the lead on who we hang out with and what we do each day, and every single day, he's been asking for Matt. It's been sweet watching the two of them form a relationship, and Matt has seamlessly woven his way into our daily lives.

I'm so glad that Elliot thinks as highly of Matt as I do, because all I want to do is be around him, too. The magnetic pull that I've always felt toward him isn't just from his personality anymore. It's something far deeper, and sharing my daily life with Elliot with him has only confirmed that.

Alright, guys, one more time, and then we should head back!" I call. "It's getting late."

"Okay!" Elliot calls from the bike. He makes one last run, where he successfully makes the longest stretch on his own.

"Woo hoo! Way to go, E!" I call.

"That was a great run, Elliot," Matt says, pushing the bike by the handlebars while Elliot walks next to me. "We just need to work a little bit more on balance, but that'll come with practice."

Elliot sneaks his little hand in mine, and it sends a rush of happiness through my body. His hand fits there.

It belongs there.

Matt secures the bike onto the bike rack outside the apartment building by fastening the lock. Then, he holds the door open for us as we head up the stairs. We walk right past Matt's apartment and head toward mine.

"Alright, buddy," I say, giving his hand a little squeeze before letting go so we can take our shoes off inside. "Why don't you go brush your teeth."

He runs down the hall, setting in motion the nightly routine the three of us have fallen into. Elliot always brushes his teeth, changes into his pajamas, and then Matt and I join him in his room.

"What book will it be tonight?" Matt asks, having a seat on the corner of Elliot's bed while I plop down in the bean bag chair.

"This one." Elliot hands him a book about race cars before climbing under the covers. Matt reads through the book, even doing it a second time when Elliot begs him. I have a feeling he could ask Matt to read it fifty times, and he would say yes.

"Goodnight, bud. I'll see you tomorrow," Matt says, giving him a high-five. "I'll meet you out there," he whispers to me before heading out of his room.

"Goodnight, Elliot," I say.

"Goodnight," he whispers, eyelids already starting to look heavy. I watch him, as I do every night, counting my blessings that life led me to him, until his soft snores fill the room.

I climb out of the chair and quietly tiptoe out the door. I find Matt in the kitchen, wiping down the kitchen counter to clean up the dinner mess from earlier, the quiet hum of the dishwasher running next to the sink. I come up behind him, wrapping my arms around his middle, hands resting flat against the hard ridges of his stomach.

He sets the rag into the sink, then grabs my arms while he twists around, keeping me in place until I'm firmly pressed against his stomach, his hands resting on my hips.

"We make a good team, don't we?" I say, holding his gaze as his eyes find mine.

"We do," he whispers, bringing his lips closer to mine. I push mine against his, squeezing him tighter, relishing in the butterflies that always wake up low in my belly when I kiss him. Eventually, he breaks away, running his hands up my back.

"I have to head back to my place," he says quietly. "My shift at the bar starts at nine." His eyes pierce mine with such intensity it almost takes my breath away. It's moments like this that I know, without a doubt, that I'm head over heels for this guy. Regardless of what the future brings, I'm confident that we can figure it out together—that I want to.

Whatever compromises, promises, and serious commitments a life with him would entail, I'm all in. I really always have been. Judging by the way his eyes are smoldering into mine, I know he agrees. The way he felt about me was never a question and never faltered, even when our lives became complicated. I just needed to catch up, which he waited patiently for me to do.

"I have something I've been wanting to tell you," I tell him softly, not breaking eye contact. I suddenly can't stand the thought of him leaving tonight without hearing this.

"What's that?" His eyes soften, and the way he looks at me makes it easy to say what I'm about to say.

"I'm completely in love with you, Matthew Swanson," I tell him softly and sincerely, meaning it with every fiber of my being. His face breaks into a huge grin, and he presses his forehead to mine, gripping me tighter.

"Finally… I love you, too."

EPILOGUE

PAIGE

One year later

"Welcome to phase three of this Ultimate Swanson Family Day of Fun!" Matt says as we come to an open stretch of sand, dropping our multiple bags and gear that comes with us when we travel anywhere these days.

"Beach activities," he announces, directing his attention to Elliot. "We'll start with playing a couple intense games of tic-tac-toe in the sand, then we'll do a bucket race—see who can spill the least amount of water while running from point A to point B. Lastly, a sandcastle competition. Mom and Noelle will be the judges." He gestures at me and the eight-month-old little girl wrapped snugly around me in a sling wrap.

"Okay! I'll draw a tic-tac-toe grid in the sand!" Elliot shouts, scrambling to find a stick to use. I watch him in wonder and once again marvel at my life, as I've done often this past year.

Once Matt and I decided to be all in, it didn't take us long to really live that sentiment to the fullest. We were more than ready to start our lives together, and we wanted to do it right.

Matt proposed in the middle of my living room with vases of flowers covering almost every square inch of the room. Elliot, Mia, and John were hiding down the hallway, and the look of excitement on Elliot's face just made the moment that much more perfect.

We had a small legal ceremony at the courthouse soon after and then started the process of legally adopting Elliot immediately. We didn't want to waste time by planning a big wedding. We wanted each other. That was all that mattered.

He's been officially ours for the last five months, and nothing has ever felt more meant to be. Of course, it wasn't all easy. We had our fair share of hard days. Elliot had sporadic nightmares and was slow to warm up in most situations. But we were consistently patient with him, never faltering in our support of him, and he's come such a long way. Watching him gleefully run around and laugh with Matt reminds me of how far he's come.

Noelle eventually joined our lives, turning our worlds upside down with beautiful chaos the way newborns do. She's added so much joy and laughter to our family dynamic, and Alicia has been an absolute dream to co-parent with.

My parents and Caleb flew out for the wedding and again when Noelle was born. They're excited to be grandparents and are actually looking into buying a vacation home somewhere on Oahu.

Matt, Elliot, and I even made a trip back to Minnesota before Noelle was born to visit my parents and to say goodbye to Harley, who didn't have much time left. I still miss that darn dog so much. It's on our five-year plan to get a dog of our own. Elliot's already been begging for one.

I unwrap Noelle and sit her down on a beach towel under the umbrella Matt set up, handing her a couple toys to play with.

Elliot rushes over to stick her pacifier in her mouth and rub her back, then runs back to Matt. He's such an attentive, caring big brother, and it makes my heart melt every time I see them interacting.

Matt pulls his shirt off and tosses it to me with a wink.

"Look at that dad bod!" I tease him, admiring the well-defined muscles that are the absolute opposite of a dad bod. I watch with a smile as they start their games, and once again, I'm struck by how much I love Matt. Every single second of my life with him is more than I ever dreamed it would be, and I'm proud of the way he's stepped up as a husband and father. He shifted seamlessly into being a dad—and a great one, no less.

Of course, we still have plenty of help from his family. His sisters still show up unannounced, bringing food and gifts for the kids. The way they've accepted Elliot as one of their own has me feeling forever in debt to them.

Shortly after we got married, Marty asked to meet with Matt. He confided in him that he wasn't up for running the bar anymore, but he didn't want to sell it to just anybody. He offered the bar to Matt, and when Matt said he couldn't afford to buy it, Marty set up a payment plan and handed over the keys. He's been working so hard to fix that place up and turn it into the bar of his dreams, and we're only a couple payments away from it being officially ours. Seeing him feel so fulfilled in his work life is inspiring.

I started teaching third grade at Honu Elementary last fall while Elliot started second grade. It's been great to be able to be at the same school, able to eat lunch together and check in throughout the day, and we're both thriving there. He's come a long way with his confidence and work ethic, and I could not be more proud.

My phone dings with a text from Mia.

Mia: Still on for Scrabble tonight?

Paige: Yes. See you at 6!

John and Mia have been coming by a few times a week for a game night. Quinn sometimes joins us if she's not off on an adventure or traveling to some far off-destination none of us have ever heard of. I admire that girl and her zest for life.

Elliot absolutely loves game night, and I love spending time with our friends. When John and Mia got married on the beach last month, they asked both Elliot and Noelle to be a part of it. Elliot was the ring bearer, and Hazel pulled Noelle down the aisle in a wagon. They were the cutest flower girls I've ever seen.

"Hey, Mom, can you hold this for me?" Elliot hands me his hat, and I take it, smiling back at him. It took him a while to call me mom, and obviously, I didn't pressure him, but the night we officially adopted him, he whispered, "Goodnight, Mom," as he was falling asleep. It still feels surreal every time he says it. Being called mom by him, bonus-mom by Noelle, and wife by Matt is all I'll ever need.

I think back to when I first came here on summer break last year, when I couldn't have possibly anticipated the turn my life would take, or how Matt and I would somehow manage to work through our circumstances and pull together this unconventional life that is absolutely perfect in every way. I'll always think back on that summer break as the summer that forever changed my life. The summer I found my family.

The End

ALSO BY MEGAN REINKING

The Hawaiian Getaway Series

The Ohana Cottage

The Summer Break

ACKNOWLEDGMENTS

First, thank you to you, reader! Thank you for reading my books and supporting this dream of mine! I had so much fun writing this story, and I hope that you love it as much as I do!

Thank you to Nick for your constant support and for celebrating every minor success with me. I love you. Thank you to my kids for telling me how proud you are of me, and cheering me on - even though you aren't allowed to read my books until you're older :) This wouldn't be nearly as much fun without a house full of love to share it all with.

Thank you to my Mom for reading every single piece of work I send you, and for being one of my biggest cheerleaders!

Thank you to Lindsey for beta reading this story as I wrote chapter by chapter, and for giving me invaluable feedback along the way! Your friendship and encouragement means so much to me!

Thank you to Jamie for jumping on board last minute to beta read. Your enthusiasm and excitement for The Summer Break was greatly appreciated, and immensely helpful! I'm forever grateful that you said yes because I gained not only a phenomenal beta reader, but most importantly a friend.

Thank you to my editor, cover designer and everyone else who had a hand in making this book come to life. I am so grateful for you!

Lastly, thank you to all of my family members and friends for your continued support and excitement. It truly means the world to me!!

ABOUT THE AUTHOR

Megan Reinking is a wife and mother who lives in Minnesota, where she spends her days reading, writing or chauffeuring her three children around town. She's a homebody who loves quiet, lazy days and connecting with family and friends.

CPSIA information can be obtained
at www.ICGtesting.com
Printed in the USA
LVHW050806090523
746487LV00003B/384